Sahitya Akademi & Jnanpith Award Winner

INDIRA Goswami

five novellas about ~~women~~

Translated from Assamese by Dibyajyoti Sarma

THORNBIRD
NIYOGI BOOKS

Published by
NIYOGI BOOKS
Block D, Building No. 77,
Okhla Industrial Area, Phase-I,
New Delhi-110 020, INDIA
Tel: 91-11-26816301, 26818960
Email: niyogibooks@gmail.com
Website: www.niyogibooksindia.com

Editor: K.E. Priyamvada
Design: Shashi Bhushan Prasad
Cover design: Pinaki De

ISBN: 978-93-91125-07-3
Publication: 2021

Printed at: Niyogi Offset Pvt. Ltd., New Delhi, India

Contents

Introduction

CONTEXTUALISING INDIRA GOSWAMI

Is Indira Goswami still relevant? The answer is an empathic yes—both as an Assamese writer of influence and a woman writer of importance. She blazed the trail by tackling hitherto taboo issues in her writings (widowhood, female sexuality, caste/class oppression) and remains one of the few writers to do so with the clear-eyed vision of a seasoned storyteller and the zealousness of an activist.

In Goswami's writing, the personal is always political. She wrote what she saw and what she saw was an unjust world at war with itself within the bounds of patriarchy. Her vision of the world was the universal desire to transcend the norms of society and live the idealised individual life. While her characters usually fail to achieve this, what makes Goswami's writing important is this indomitable desire, this constant struggle to rise above one's station. Thus, as long as there's societal strife, as long as women struggle to assert their rights, Indira Goswami will remain relevant.

In the context of Assamese literature, Goswami was both an outlier and a champion of Assamese literary tradition. On the one hand, Goswami broke the mould of the contemporary Assamese writing by foregrounding characters and issues hitherto untouched by her peers (her depiction of frank sexuality and her experimentation with the language was indeed something new). On the other hand, she remained a part of the established Assamese literary tradition (starting from Madhava Kandali, who translated the *Ramayan* into Assamese), with a focus on rural dynamics and literature as a vehicle of social change.

The first Assamese woman writer (and second Assamese person so far) to win the highest national literary award, the Jnanpith, in 2000, Goswami can be seen as one of the early women writers from Assam who exclusively focused on women characters and discussed female sexuality in direct, no-nonsense terms, thus paving the way for other authors like Arupa Patangia Kalita and Purobi Bormudoi. Yet, Goswami's thematic concerns far exceeded any other author's from Assam. Her writings range from the inner workings of a Vaishnavite monastery or the Christian missionaries, to the widows of Vrinadavan or the sadhus of Kamakhya temple, as also to workers' daily struggles in Madhya Pradesh, to psycho-sexual explorations by the youth in a city like Guwahati. She wrote unabashedly about her loneliness and depression ('those days I used to carry vials of sleeping pills in my bag', she writes in her autobiography) and her connection to the disadvantaged (her concern for her Sikh driver during the 1984 riots described by her in *Pages Stained with Blood and Dust*). More than that, with her redbindi adorned forehead, kohl-lined eyes and ever-smiling face, she remains an icon, the beloved Mamoni Baideu for a generation of writers both in Assamese and English.

While primarily a fiction writer, Goswami has never shied away from foregrounding her ideology and beliefs in her writing and her public life. She has written candidly about her depression and suicidal tendencies following the death of her husband. Also, she wrote uninhibitedly about clandestine affairs, female desire and misguided masculinities. Later, she expressed her angst against animal sacrifice at the Kamakhya temple in Guwahati in her creative and journalistic writings. Her active participation to bring the leaders of the banned outfit ULFA to the negotiation table can be seen in much of her non-fiction writing (she was the only civilian who had direct access to the exiled ULFA leader, Paresh Barua).

While Goswami is usually seen as a feminist writer focusing on the themes of women's emancipation, the locus of her writing intersects in the primal conflict between man and woman, with religion and patriarchy fueling this difference by denying women their sexual autonomy and by pushing men towards a false sense of hetero-masculinity. While the 'single woman' (usually a widow, a reflection of Goswami's own predicament) remains the centre of her writings, irrespective of settings—be it the village in lower Assam where she grew up, or Vrindavan, or Madhya Pradesh or Delhi—Goswami problematises her heroines by giving them sexual agency that runs counter to the societal expectations. The conflict arising from this clash or the collision between what is deviant and what is rendered normal in a social space is what makes Goswami's writings unique and unprecedented. This inevitably results in violence, both imagined and real ('peeling the skin alive' is one of Goswami's favourite expressions; in a story, a Brahmin woman would rather abort a foetus than carry a lower-caste man's seed, in another a sadhu would sacrifice himself rather than allow animal sacrifice), but it also helps break the status quo. Neither are her women nor her men, villains. Both are victims of the oppressive structures of society/religion.

Goswami wrote exclusively in Assamese under the pseudonym Mamoni Raisom Goswami. She also translated some of her own works into English. We can further contend that Goswami's life and her very act of writing have been shaped as a series of translations: Goswami constantly dealt with translation as an act of defiance, as an act of ushering the change and as an act of negotiating space. She was an attractive young widow who steadfastly fended off advances of suitors and refused to remarry. She was born in an orthodox religious family, yet married outside, against her family's wishes. At a time, when Assamese writing was trying to shed its rural roots to focus on the problems of burgeoning towns and cities, Goswami wrote about far-flung places, about the workers' struggles in Kashmir and Madhya Pradesh and about the plight of widows in Vrindavan. She also remains one of the few major Assamese writers to openly write about a homosexual protagonist.

Later, during her research on the *Ramayan*, she studied the various translations of the text, which remained a lifelong passion. As faculty at Delhi University, she met North Indian authors writing in Hindi, Punjabi and Urdu and absorbed the currents of the prevailing literatures. At the height of the Assam movement in the 1980s, Goswami translated the Hindi poet Sarveshwar Dayal Saxena's poem, '*Desh Kagaj Par Bana Naksha Nahin Hota*'. A large number of her stories (such as 'Delhi, 5 November 1991'; 'Ishwari's Doubts and Desires' and 'Snake-skin Shoes') are exclusively set in North India and a large number of Hindi words are used by her. She popularised the Urdu/Hindi word 'Khoonkhaar' (violent/cruel) in Assamese. On the other hand, the setting of her fictional world in Assam remained restricted to either Guwahati or the region of Chaygaon in lower Assam, where the language is a dialect of the Kamrupiya, which itself is a dialect of Assamese. That is why some of her Assamese stories contain glossaries.

The context of each novella, the reasons for each selection, and some of their nuances are explained in this chapter. For some insights into the translation, please see the Translator's Note and for the meanings of specific words or terms, please refer to the Glossary.

BREAKING THE BEGGING BOWL

The story has a strong allegorical context. The title refers to the wretchedness of the situation, which is so bad that the begging bowl, perhaps the last material possession of a beggar, breaks and the beggar is left with nothing.

'Breaking the Begging Bowl', is a grand tragedy, something on the lines of Bertolt Brecht's *Mother Courage and Her Children*, and J.M. Synge's *Riders to the Sea*, where, in the midst of the demands of patriarchy and an oppressive society, and destiny's cruel joke, stands a woman, battered and bruised, yet struggling to survive until the end.

This woman is Phuleshwari, a lower-caste woman in the rural parts of Kamrup district in Assam. As the story begins, she is accused of doing something she did not do. Then her husband dies and things go downhill from there. Her elder daughter is widowed; her son joins the burgeoning insurgency movement and her younger daughter grows up to be a loner. To make matters worse, a piece of land belonging to her daughter's dead husband is grabbed by an opportunist leader of the community.

Indira Goswami tells this story of singular tragedy with stark prose, incisive observation and visceral imagery, where, while she empathises with every one of her characters, she spares none. Instead of taking sides and making comments, she lets the readers confront the reality on their own. She does so with the expert use of a host of literary and stylistic devices, such as the use of the local fauna not just to underscore the region where the story is set, but also to highlight the emotional state of her characters. The Chaygaon region, where the story is set, is traditionally known for its fertile land, washed over not just by the mighty

Brahmaputra, but also by its various tributaries. Fish are aplenty here, and thus naturally, Goswami makes generous use of fish imagery. She also uses the onomatopoeic sounds of the region, from the sound of falling rain to the sound of weeping, to great effect.

However, where Goswami succeeds the most, in the context of this story, is the use of the local dialect. It is said that in Assam, the spoken language changes every 14 kilometres. The local language used here is a version of the Kamrupiya dialect, widely used in its various forms, in the Brahmaputra valley of Lower Assam. The language, especially particular words, is so unique that in the original text, Goswami added a short glossary explaining the meaning of the words.

While the story doesn't refer to a particular date, from the clues available with the text (the reference to World War II and the reference to the insurgency moment), we can safely assume that the story is set between the late 1980s and early 1990s, the time when the government started its first major crackdown on the ULFA movement.

At the end, we must agree that Phuleshwari in the story is Mother Assam herself, and the problems and persecutions she faces are the problems of Assam, the struggle for the land, rural poverty, and most importantly, the insurgency movement.

THE BLOOD OF DEVIPEETH

The Kamakhya Dham, the abode of the Goddess Kamakhya, is a sixteenth-century temple set atop the Nilachal Hill, near the Brahmaputra River in Guwahati, Assam. It is a popular pilgrimage destination for the followers of the Shakti cult, who worship the Mother Goddess. The presiding manifest of the temple is a stone yoni (female generative organ). It is said that after Sati immolated herself at the sacrificial fire, Shiva roamed the world carrying her body on his shoulder. To save the world, Vishnu started dismembering the body with his chakra. During the process, the Goddess's yoni fell into the spot where the temple resides. It is one of the 51 Shakti Peethas related to the cult of Sati.

In the story, Padmapriya's father lives on the foothills near the long-winding stairs to the hill, called the Mekhela Ujowa Path. Mekhela Ujowa literally means 'lifting the mekhela'. It is called so because the stairs are so steep that women have to lift the hem of their lower garment to climb up.

'The Blood of Devipeeth' contains some of Goswami's pet themes, including her staunch opposition to animal sacrifice, an issue, which will find a devastating conclusion in her later masterpiece, *The Man from Chinnamasta*. Here, the Devipeeth serves as both the backdrop and the central symbol, in a story of a discarded woman finding her strength in a forbidden affair.

We do not know if something happened between Padmapriya and Shambhudev inside the cave, and frankly, it doesn't matter. Yet, the haunting scene, where Padmapriya follows Shambhudev to the darkness of the cave to find the golden flower, is the central motif of the text, very much like the Marabar Cave scene in E.M. Forster's

A Passage to India. The only difference is that the experience gives her the courage to stand up for herself. However, nowhere is this use of a central image to support the narrative more evident than in 'The Blood of Devipeeth'. Here, the realistic narrative is broken into pieces to give way for the symbolic one. We scarcely know what transpired between Padmapriya and her estranged husband. What we know is that Padmapriya is lost and must find her way. She starts her journey as the sacrificial buffalo (hence the affinity with the scimitar-wielding Shambhudev), and ends up as the enlightened one, who witnesses the Goddess dancing.

Thus, the scenes involving the buffalo sacrifice, the white Kunda flower and the pilgrims climbing up the hill, which Goswami uses repeatedly like a poetic refrain, must be read both as a realistic description of the surroundings and Padmapriya's inner turmoil. Here, the only way we can enter into the inner world of Padmapriya's mind is how she interacts with her surroundings. This is why she wants to sacrifice herself like a buffalo. This is why she becomes obsessed with finding the white flowers. This is why her transgressions with both Seng, the dwarf, and Shambhudev, the man who performs the animal sacrifice.

This also illuminates how Goswami uses the colours white and red to signify the process through which her heroine will come to terms with her reality. Padmapriya is discarded by her husband because of a white vitiligo mark on her back. After the initial trauma, she takes refuge in the power of the Goddess.

There is a legend attached to the image of the Goddess dancing naked on the full moon night. It was said that the Goddess danced naked in the temple on the moonlit night and the chief priest was the only person who was allowed to witness this divine manifestation. When the news of this miracle reached the king of the Koch dynasty, Naranarayan, he expressed a desire to witness the dance. He was the king, so the chief priest could not deny him. On the next full moon night, the king stood outside the temple and peeped through a hole to witness the dance. The Goddess was understandably angry. She struck the priest blind and ordered the king never to set foot in the temple again. To atone for his sins, king Naranarayan rebuilt the temple as it stands today, and until this day, his descendants do not visit the temple.

DELHI, 5 NOVEMBER 1991

Not much of Indira Goswami's writing on Delhi has been translated into English. This is the reason why '5 November 1991' has been included here.

The title refers to the 1991 Delhi hooch tragedy, which killed 199 people. Most of those who died were casual labourers and rickshaw-pullers, who had consumed Karpoor Asav or sura, a so-called ayurvedic medicine. The liquor was manufactured by a firm called Karnal Pharmacy, based in Ghaziabad in Uttar Pradesh. Tests confirmed that the substance contained methyl alcohol.

Goswami narrates the horrors of this singular tragedy from the point of view of a woman, who starts as an outsider eyewitness, before the devastating effects of the tragedy hit home. Yet, as it is evident in all her stories, Goswami cannot be satisfied with telling just one strand of the narrative. The novella follows two different narrative strands, which merges at one point with devastating results. Here, Vimala is a stand-in for the author to describe the life of the daily-wage labourers and the victims of the hooch tragedy, and yet, Vimala gets her own story as well, the story of a woman trapped in a patriarchal world, a world which looks at her as a sex object.

ISHWARI'S DOUBTS AND DESIRES

Besides being a fiction writer of repute, Indira Goswami was a respected scholar of *Ramayan* literature, who wrote a groundbreaking comparative study of Tulsidas's *Ramcharitmanas* and the fourteenth-century Assamese *Ramayan* by Madhava Kandali, called *Ramayana from Ganga to Brahmaputra*.

Following a particularly difficult time in her life after the death of her husband, Indira Goswami's teacher Upendra Chandra Lekharu persuaded her to come to Vrindavan in Uttar Pradesh, and pursue research on *Ramayan*, as a way to deal with her inner turmoil. Her experiences as a widow as well as a researcher finds expression in her novel *Nilakanthi Braja* (*Blue-Necked Braja*, 1976), about the plight of the Radheswamis of Vrindavan. One of the issues the novel touched upon was the plight of young widows for whom companionship beyond the confines of their ashrams and fellow widows became impossible. 'Ishwari's Doubts and Desires' especially contains several of Goswami's pet themes—female sexuality, the plight of the widows, *Ramayan* scholarship and the politics of the epic. Goswami was also a master of creative non-fiction, as evident in her travelogue *Budhosagor Dhukhor Geisha Aru Mohammed Musa* (1980), where she combines life experiences with fictional characters. The same is the case with the first part of 'Ishwari's Doubts and Desires'. We have reason to believe that the *Ramayan* Sammelan at Janakpur mentioned in the story was a real event. There are references to a number of real life personalities, from Camille Bulcke to Acharya Khemraj Keshav Sharma. The journey from Delhi to Janakpur in Nepal, as Ishwari experiences in the story, has almost a documentary quality.

The story is about the struggle between the human desire for love and spiritual commitment. Ishwari, a widow, is in love with Dharma Bahadur, but cannot really express it. She feels guilty about her feelings but cannot really help it. The story ends with a devastating irony, underlining the difference between male and female privilege, where a renowned brahmachari, who has renounced women, is seen to be molesting an unwitting widow.

THE TOUCHSTONE

In the grand scheme of Goswami's fictional universe, her male characters are not essentially evil, but they suffer from a great disconnect from their other halves, the women. The men cannot enter the interior worlds of the women and fail to love them the way the women want to be loved. In Goswami's worldview, her men, despite their strength and power, are also trapped in the patriarchal system. In this context, it becomes easier for the men to treat women as sex objects, rather than their equals.

Dwarakanath of *The Touchstone* is a great example of this archetype, and by this, he represents all the male characters of Goswami's fictional universe. In this sense, the story is perhaps the closest Goswami came to writing a love story from the point of view of a male character. Understandably, it must end in tragedy.

Unlike most of Goswami's stories, where geography plays an important role, in *The Touchstone*, we are not certain where the story is set. There is a reference to a river and a forest. There is a reference to Barsana, which is a place in Mathura. But the reference to rain and the names of the women characters suggest that it may be Assam as well. There is hardly any reference to the local fauna to identify the place, which is perhaps a deliberate attempt, as most of the story takes place in the interiors of the mind of Dwarakanath.

***

Translator's Note

There is a tacit expectation that Indian regional language writers should write only about the experience of the people who speak the language. This, of course, is not a fact. Hindi author Sachchidananda Hirananda Vatsyayan 'Agyeya' wrote a mesmerising story about a piece of Assamese history, 'Jayadol'. Malayalam author M.T. Vasudevan Nair has a novel called *Varanasi*. Again, in Malayalam, K.R. Meera's *Hangwoman* tells the story of a Bengali woman in Kolkata.

Indira Goswami was one of the earliest to follow the trend. She started writing while travelling with her husband to different parts of India, where he was posted as an engineer with a construction company. Thus, her first novel *Chenabor Shrot* (*The Currents of Chenab*, 1972) is set in Jammu. Her second novel *Neelkanthi Braja* (*The Blue-Necked Braja*, 1976, translated by Gayatri Bhattacharya, 2013), is set in Vrindavan, and *Mamore Dhora Tarowal* (*The Rusted Sword*, 1980) is set in Madhya Pradesh. In fact, until the publication of *Datal Hatir Une Khowa Howda* (*The Moth Eaten Howdah of a Tusker*, 1988, translated by the author), Goswami did not write a novel set in Assam, but only a handful of stories. Apart from *Tej Aru Dhulire Dhusarita Prishtha* (*Pages Stained with Blood and Dust*, 2001) not much of her writing on Delhi has been translated into English.

For Indira Goswami, writing is a precarious balance between naked emotional honesty and an evolved literary craftsmanship, which is unique even in traditional Asomiya writing. In all her writings, she balances the external narrative (the descriptions) with the emotional life of the protagonist, through whose point of view (POV) it is narrated. This POV constantly oscillates between third-person omniscient POV and third-person character POV. Goswami achieves this by using various literary and stylistic devices, like the use of violent imagery, use of dialogues with breaks, use of ellipses (…) and use of repetitions (yes, yes/no, no).

However, the most important feature of Goswami's writing is her use of the language. While she is the most inventive writer of her generation, she spent most of her writing career outside Assam. Therefore, her sentences have a different tone and cadence than a traditional Asomiya writer. She also generously uses various local dialects, especially from the region where she grew up. So much so that sometimes, even for an Asomiya reader, it is not always easy to understand the dialect.

In any translation, retaining the 'local flavour' is essential. In order to do so, I have kept most of the original words for the local flora and fauna, and other words that add to the local flavour. For example, 'paltan' is a distorted version of the word 'platoon'. A popular shopping district in Guwahati is still called Paltan Bazaar.

The rules of grammar in Asomiya are, of course, different from English. In Asomiya, it is possible to move between past and present tense without losing the sense of time. This is not possible in English. Hence, where required, I have turned the whole text into a past tense narrative, moving between simple past and past perfect.

The same way, sounds have different onomatopoeic resonances in different languages. In the first story, I have used the local onomatopoeic sounds, not the English equivalent of them. For example, the sound of rainfall is *dhop*, *dhop*, not drip, drop.

SOME SPECIFICS OF EACH NOVELLA

Breaking the Begging Bowl: My first problem was how to represent the dialect, which is spoken on the north side of the Brahmaputra River in Kamrup District. While translating, I have retained some of the words, especially words which cannot be translated, or which, if translated, would sound very odd. When the words have occurred twice, I have used a translation as well as the original.

For example, the approximately correct translation of the word 'beti' used in the story is not the Hindi translation (daughter), but the English word 'wench'. I have used both the words. Same is with the abuse words like *barabhateri*, which means someone who has twelve husbands, and *dhekura*, meaning stray dog, and *bhithi utha*, someone whose entire clan is extinct.

The Blood of Devipeeth: Depending on the plot, Goswami's writing can be viscerally direct or maddeningly opaque. She is one of the few writers of her generation who could write about any issue, especially issues which were usually taboo in literature of the time, like women's sexuality, with a frankness that is direct and disturbing.

Indira Goswami is a master storyteller of opaque emotions, where human feelings find its manifestation in the natural world. This is one such work. Nothing is explained here. What we get is a series of scenes and a series of vivid images, and we are invited to recreate Padmapriya's life with these tools.

Delhi, 5 November 1991: The original story contains a large number of Hindi dialogues, without offering a translation. The premise is that the Asomiya readers would understand the Hindi dialogues, written in Asomiya script. In the translation, I have kept some of the Hindi dialogues intact, not only to retain the flavour of the original text, but also to showcase Goswami's tremendous skill in writing Hindi.

Unlike the stories set in Assam, which are filled with imagery from the natural world, the current story mostly uses abstract imagery, which translates well into English. In one place, however, the author uses atypical Asomiya imagery, which appears odd in the context of the story. In the very beginning of the story, to describe the colour of a character's skin, Goswami uses the imagery of a *bar thekera*. The fruit, *Garcinia pedunculata*, endemic to Assam, does not translate well in the context of Delhi. Thus, I have changed it to 'a ripe fruit'.

Ishwari's Doubts and Desires: The entire action of the story, in fact the entire milieu within the story is set in the Hindi belt. There are people from Uttar Pradesh, there are some foreigners, but there are no Assamese-speaking persons in the story. The story was written in Assamese, yet all the references are from texts in Sanskrit or Hindi, *Ramcharitmanas* being a big influence.

In all likelihood, Goswami conceived the story in Hindi and wrote it in Assamese. In the translation, we have converted the Hindi sentences transliterated in Assamese by Goswami into Roman Hindi, followed by English in brackets. As a discerning reader would notice, the writing follows the same style evident in 'The Blood of Devipeeth'. Thus, the same translation methods have been employed.

There were very few inherently Assamese expressions used in the novel. So, I have kept the expressions 'Hari, Hari' and 'Issh' just to indicate the original source. Goswami's uses of ellipses are also retained. I have used the names as written/spoken in Assamese. So, Ram instead of Rama, and so on.

The Touchstone: This is the most straightforward text in the selection. The translator did not have to make any radical choices. Goswami's propensity to use ellipses (…) is visible here as well and the translation maintains this. There is one tree mentioned prominently in the text and instead of using the original Assamese name, as I have done in case of the other stories, I have kept the English equivalent, so that the flow is not disturbed. However, towards the end, where two swear words are used by Snehalata, I have kept the original, to maintain the force of her anger, to make it more impactful.

***

Breaking the Begging Bowl

Phuleshwari had promised herself on a number of occasions—she would never come and stand next to the Dhaleshwari River again. During the last agitation, at this very spot, she had found the dead bodies of two students. Scorched by bullets, their bodies lay in a heap, as if they were two deer killed by hunters. Oh! And, were there more memories…

Leaving her house and brushing her teeth with the twig of a sara tree, Phuleshwari walked towards Dhaleshwari. Often she would tell herself, she would never go visiting the riverbank. Yet, her legs would invariably bring her to the same spot.

Standing near the pipal tree with a giant hollow, next to the river, Phuleshwari saw several military vehicles pass by, blowing dust on the pebbled road (these had increased ever since the government crackdown on the insurgency movement, led by the United Liberation Front of Assam, in the early 1990s). In the ensuing racket, the egrets on the tree flew away.

…Phuleshwari had forgotten many things. Yet, some stories were ever-present, like rock carvings on her mind.

The story of the military was one such story—a story that filled her heart with dark soot.

After the vehicles left, the smell that pervaded the air remained the same; the smell of German grass and petrol. Forty years ago, the same smell would float everywhere in Kakabori. Was it just forty years? Or more? No, no, she did not remember. Perhaps, it was more. Six or seven years more. That ungainly smell would pervade the atmosphere, making the people of Kakabori forget the soft scents of bakul, bhumi champa and even the kagazi lemon flowers.

Phuleshwari walked toward the point where the three roads converged and sat under the old pipal tree next to the road. Ah! Blowing dust, they just passed by her. Should she walk a little ahead to check? Yes, where did they go? Those military vehicles?

Usually, Phuleshwari woke up before anyone else in Kakabori. For sometime now, the family was going through such monetary hardship that Phuleshwari had to go and collect mati-kaduri, khutura, kochu and other leafy edibles from the roadside to cook for three persons twice a day. After rinsing her mouth in the river, she would usually finish collecting her vegetables. The neighbours were aware that she had now started eyeing their vegetable patches as well. Just the other day, there was such brouhaha after two gourds were stolen from the roof of the garden of the fisherman's house next to Dhaleshwari.

Crossing the road, she went down to the river through the 'leak' made by the wheels of the bullock carts and washed her face and hands. As she started to wipe her face with the dirty gatala that lay on her bosom, she started to shiver. … Yes, this time winter had arrived before the month of Magh. Or was it because she was getting old?

The fog enwrapped the hills faraway. On the bholuka bamboo grove on the other side, the dewdrops lay like a flowery spider's net.

…There was a *hok, hok* sound amidst the sickle-like grasses. It was the sound of a dauk. Amidst the green grasses, Phuleshwari noticed the black wings of the bird. Hiding her hands behind her gatala, she stood there for a while, waiting for a chance. But was it easy to catch a short-tailed dauk? Footsteps did not matter; they would fly away even at the scent of a human. She had tried to catch dauks next to Dhaleshwari numerous times. She knew how delicious the flesh of the bird was. Even now, she would crave for a taste of the meat, even when she was as poor as the famine-affected.

…Slowly, it dawned. Like the flesh of a rabbit cut into nibbles, scarlet pieces of cloud surrounded the sun. Oh! The military vehicles were back. It was time to return home. But no, she left the riverbank and sat under the peepal tree with the giant hollow. These days, when she walked, her kneecaps made a *kat, kat* sound. Yet, she waited with anticipation, there might be more vehicles coming.

The burden of her age could not crush that anticipation. Memory was like the golden deer. Mysterious. Somewhere in her flesh, the golden deer continued to endure. It thrived despite the storm and the lash of the whip, and in a moment, it appeared, dazzling the vision. Phuleshwari felt like that. From the dark recesses of her heart, in a fraction, the deer jumped out.

....It was 48 years ago. Kinaram Satriya had married her from Kaldiya and brought her to the banks of Dhaleshwari. That year, the Gohain Adhikari of the Kakabori Satra, Hridayananda Deb Adhikari, had gone to visit his disciples on the banks of the Kaldiya River. Kinaram was an orphan. He would farm on a piece of land belonging to Gohain Hridayananda. Kinaram Satriya was a man of strength. Why in Kakabori, in the entire south side of the river, there was not a single man as handsome as Kinaram.

...Phuleshwari daubed the corners of her eyes with her gatala. Yes, she was brought here from Kaldiya with great hope. Kinaram would follow Gohain Hridayananda Deb everywhere, like a shadow. After returning from the field, freshening up and changing his clothes, and after having a snack of gura-xandah (ground flattened rice, eaten with milk or water and jaggery), he would walk towards the residence of Gohain Mahaprabhu. Yes. Yes. Most of the time, Phuleshwari was alone. The day, when that terrible incident took place, that day too, Phuleshwari was alone.

Though Kinaram had asked, the old bhakat, Dhaniram, who would usually stand guard in the household in the absence of Kinaram, was missing that day. On other days, he would come before dusk and spread his bed on the floor next to the bhakheri, where grains were stored. Sometimes, he would start preparing kani (opium) next to the smouldering fire of rice husks, in the dhekhal, where the dheki, the wooden instrument used to pound rice grains, was placed.

That day he was not there. There was a function at someone's house in Dompul. There, it started raining. He could not return home during the night. Even Dahi Mistiri's daughter, who would sometimes give her company when Kinaram was not home, could not come that night because of the rain.

It was a terrible rain. Water dripped from the thatched roof of the house and created a puddle next to her bed. She had never heard that kind of noise from clouds and thunder in Kakabori. She lay on the bed and listened to the hard sound of the robab tenga falling behind the house. She was terrified that the tamarind tree that grew next to the house would be uprooted and fall on her roof. She was trembling with fear. She waited impatiently for the rain to stop.

Suddenly, the deafening sound of a thunder burst shook her up and she fell on the floor with her face down.

Just then, she heard someone knock on the door. She was not sure if the storm was making the noise or if someone was actually there. She perked up her ears and sat there in a trance.

But just for a moment; someone opened the door with a kick of his boots. ...In front of her, like a wild animal, drenched in water, stood a soldier, with a gun in his hand.

A soldier?

Yes! Yes! A soldier!

A gun in his hand. The water that dripped from his body made the floor of her hut muddy.

Yes, yes, it was the dress of a paltan, a hat on his head, a gun in his hand. A pair of boots smeared with mud. …He saw her and quickly closed the door. Immediately, placing the gun next to the wall, he tried to murmur something. No, no, there was no attack on her. He did not have the look of a crude rapist. He looked like someone in trouble. …The sound of the rain had not stopped yet. Quivering with fear, she kept thinking just one thing, if she could just reach the door, she would be able to flee. …No, no, it was impossible. The man was standing just in front of the door and he was strong. Now, what was he doing? He removed his boots, then his soaked shirt, which was plastered onto his skin. With the nozzle of his gun, he pushed the items towards her and told her something, using wild gestures.

Phuleshwari now knew for certain that a runaway soldier was standing in front of her. His face was soft. He was very young.

Leaving the boots and the shirt, and carrying the gun on his shoulders, he left the way he had come, in the middle of the rain, with naked feet.

…Slowly, the intensity of the rain lessened. She got up from the floor. …What would she do? What would she do now with the shirt and the mud-smeared boots? They lay in front of her like terrible evidences of a murder. This evidence could turn her into a criminal as well. Yes, yes, it could turn her into a criminal. Though illiterate, this much Phuleshwari knew. Though young, this much she knew.

There were some strands of German grass and some leaves of the bhatara tree on the boots. The shirt lay crumpled like a dry banana leaf.

What would she do? ...Would she hide them near the dhekhal? No, no, everyone would see them there. Then where? In the bhakheri?

A soldier's boots in the bhakheri?

Somewhere, her heart crumbled. As she was still wondering what to do, there was a sudden convulsion. The entire village woke up to the sound of bamboo sticks and heavy boots, as if the entire camp of the paltan was there... crossing the Three-Road Chowk, they were marching towards the village.

...Phuleshwari, who was about to step out, took shelter inside her hut again. What was it? What was happening? Shouting and screaming, the party of the paltans went ahead and ransacked each and every household in the village. There was the *dham, dham* sound of the boots and the clunky sounds of the household items being thrown out. Hearing the screams of the young children and the howling of the women, who had stepped away from the paltans like grasshoppers, Phuleshwari started to tremble. She thought of taking the items to the backyard. She thought she would do it in a jiffy. But hearing the sound of the boots on the courtyard of her house, she stood there like a statue. One of the paltans kicked open the door. The way she stood there, it was suspicious enough. Her behaviour carried the seed of suspicion. Unlike the other women, she did not run away to the verandah, screaming and shouting. One of the paltans tried to lift the bed. One of them bent down to see what was underneath the bed. Then, with a loud cry, he pulled out the pair of boots smeared with mud and the rain-soaked shirt.

...There was, meanwhile, a small gathering in her courtyard. The soldier immediately carried the boots and the shirt outside. Oh! As if a dead body had fallen in the midst of everyone present.

The gathering in the courtyard created a melee to witness the shirt and the boots of the deserter soldier.

...But it was not just the shirt and the boots of the runaway soldier, there, outside Phuleshwari's house, there lay a living soldier. It was as if everyone was trying to tear his clothes to undress him. Soon everyone's eyes were fixed on Phuleshwari, who was standing in the verandah, holding onto a post. The gaobura (village head) who was yet to wash his face in the morning, pointed his finger at her and screamed, 'Speak, swear and speak, did the paltan enter your house before?'

Holding onto the post in the verandah, Phuleshwari was so surprised that she could not utter a single word.

Now, all the important people in the village shouted together: 'Tell us the truth. The paltans are waiting. Speak, aapi, speak.'

Even then, nothing came out of her mouth. An old woman, who had blacked her teeth with jamuki, revealing her teeth like a beaten fox, cried: 'You, consort of twelve husbands, you have brought shame to the whole village. Confess. Confess the truth. I think you are a woman used by everyone.'

Another woman shouted, 'What the public did not do when they found that Bhikhu Koomar's daughter from Dakhala grew a tummy with a paltan! Tell us. Swear.'

Confused, she sat next to the post and started to weep.

Daringly, the soldiers again went inside the hut. The bed, the mattress, ugha-chereki, peera, pots and pans, nothing was spared. …No, there was nothing else. They only found a saucepan with a handle, used by the soldiers. …Those saucepans with handles were found not only in her house. Made like an elephant's head, this kind of saucepan was in everyone's house. The paltans knew that those saucepans, used by the soldiers, were to be found even in the kitchens of the gohains and the brahmins of the Kakabori Satra.

While leaving with the shirt and the boots of the runaway soldier, the paltans said in a funny-sounding Asomiya, 'We will come often to take stock of the situation. If anyone of you can find any information about the runaway soldier, inform us immediately. We will reward you.'

Making distinct sounds with their boots, the paltans took a short cut through the jungle filled with bholuka bamboo, German grass, aera plants and godhuli gopal flowers and reached the main road.

One by one, the gathering crowd started to disperse from Phuleshwari's courtyard. Nobody came and stood next to her.

Even the women, who were late for their morning household duties, failed to talk to her and find out the truth. After all, she was not from Kakabori. She was from the North side of the Brahmaputra River. She did not have any friends here.

While leaving, they said: 'Beti, barabhateri, she has destroyed the reputation of the village.'

'Now, will the paltans leave the young girls in the village alone?'

'Now, will the young girls be able to go shopping to Three-Chowk Mirja? The wench has shown the way.'

Nothing had been forgotten. Everything was crystal clear in memory.

...Did she really see that runaway soldier somewhere before? While going to the haat in Mirja? On the riverbed on the day of Suwari festival? Yes, yes, even when the paltans visited this side, looking for ducks and chickens, she had never seen a face like that.

After her bath, she entered the hut and standing next the upturned bed, she could not move. What a terrible thing had happened? What a terrible thing!

One day, the Babaji, who had come down from the Garo Hills and was staying at the temple under the bakul tree, had said: 'These guys, who are staying in tents near the river, these military people, they themselves do not know whom they are going to kill. They were kidnapped and were forced to join the paltan. They will have to shoot at whoever the Gora government points their fingers at. Now, you tell me, if you do not have a fire inside you, can you murder a human being? You will have to make Gora government your God. You will have to set fire on yourself. Then only you will be able to fight a war with guns. Not everyone can do this. Haven't you heard a paltan from Mirja had run away? They finally caught him the jungles of Ukiam. …Yes, yes, these are runaway paltans. Paltans who failed to kill and then ran.'

In spite of her tumultuous state of mind, Phuleshwari felt a kind of affinity for the runaway soldier. …No, no, he did not even look at her properly. In a hurry, he had just readied himself to run.

Then, there was a piercing cry to break her heart into two: 'Oh, my dear mother, why did he come and suck my life blood away?'

… Everything, Phuleshwari remembered everything.

The Gohain Mahaprabhu had returned from visiting his disciples in the North. Kinaram was one of those boys who helped the Gohain get down from the elephant at the Three-Road Chowk and then carried him to the Satra in a palanquin.

At Three-Road Chowk, he heard how the paltan's clothes were discovered from under the bed in his house.

On top of it, on his shoulder, he carried a festering wound. After reaching home, like a man suffering from brain fever, he lay on the bed. Blood and pus from the wound on his shoulder fell on the pillow. Looking for a straight answer, he asked her. 'For how long were you seeing the paltan? Speak, since when had he been coming here?'

With a straight face, she too answered, 'He came just once on the rainy night. I had not seen him before.'

Without blinking, Kinaram looked at Phuleshwari for a long time. Then he got up with a start, like a man bitten by a snake. 'With so many houses around, how come he decided to come and hide under your bed? …Or is this the same tale as that daughter of Bhikhu Koomar from Dakhala…'

He was a young man; suddenly blood rushed to his brain. Like a wild buffalo, with a mad intensity, he grabbed her hair. He dragged her to the courtyard and then started to kick her.

There was a skirmish. The courtyard, once again, was filled with people. At that very moment, Phuleshwari's father, Narahari Mandal, who had came to invite his grandfather for Bihu from the north side of the river, reached the courtyard. Pleading, he grabbed Kinaram's hands: 'What are you doing? What? Do you want to kill your wife?'

With Phuleshwari, even the two-year-old Anno started to scream and cry: 'Attacked, attacked.'

They spent their days in discontent. Even then, in the span of seven years, they had three children.

…The wound, which continued to fester as Kinaram continued to carry the palanquin on the same shoulder, continued to give off blood and pus. Kinaram would fiddle with it, and make it spread and one day the wound became larger and beyond healing. Then the unhappy man passed away.

Annobala's wedding, the death of her drunk husband even before the wedding anniversary, her son—after finishing his school education and searching for a job everywhere—finally disappearing to become a terrorist, all those events took place one after another.

This happened many years later. When someone tried to clear the chegun forest on the east of Kakabori to farm the land, he found an old well used by the people going to the cremation ground. When they cleared the well, they found a human skeleton. With it, a wet, odd-shaped gun. When someone touched the wooden butt…

She heard the sound of bamboos breaking from the cremation ground. Her nostrils were filled with the stench of cauterised flesh. She got up with a start. When she had gone to the riverbank to answer nature's call, the Sun God was hiding his face on the bosom of Dhaleshwari. Now, look, like a monkey, the sun has climbed the top of the Bijuli bamboo grove in the east. Walking as fast as she could, she reached the way to the three-forked road. On the three-forked road, she met the women from Dom Para, who had come to fish in the river. Both the women screamed, 'Oi, Phuleshwari, you look so thin, like a dry bone. We heard your daughter has gone completely crazy.'

One of the women, trying to lift her mekhela with her left hand, which was already above her knees, said in a loud, ringing voice: 'That woman-smelling son of Choudhury has returned. I have seen him outside Gohain's gate.'

Before Phuleshwari could answer, the other woman beat on her ears: 'Everyone now knows that Choudhury's son is bored of your daughter. Just peel the skin of that dhekura (stray dog). You still have some teeth left. You have the strength of body, and have flesh and blood. If that dhekura had wished, he could have kept her. In the North itself, aren't there men with two women? Nobody has complained.'

Phuleshwari did not answer. The woman said again: '… Phuleshwari, your fate is barren. That's why. …Heard that the stray dog also grabbed Annobala's land…'

Phuleshwari wiped her tears with the gatala.

In a consolatory tone, the two women told her: 'Go, go, the Lord from the Other Side watches over everyone.'

They ran towards the river. For a long time, Phuleshwari could smell the stench of the women's mekhelas. Like the stench of clothes soaked for several days and then hung up to dry, their clothes had the same foul, rotten odour.

***

Returning home, Phuleshwari noticed that Annobala was sitting next to the entrance of the house having crawled all the way from the dhekhal. She must have heard that Choudhury's son had returned from the Jatra party. Even events like Annobala's widowhood or the disappearance of Hoibar could not shake Phuleshwari the way she went crazy after the Choudhury's son took away Annobala's land. They could survive for the whole year from the harvest of the land. Selling the leftover rice, they could also purchase some clothes. This land in Mora Pora Bakara was like gold.

Phuleshwari reached Annobala in a few long strides and stood next to her.

'Oi, beti, dhekuri, why suffer! Why do you suffer for him? Didn't he spit you out after chewing you like a piece of juicy sugarcane?'

In her anger, she caught hold of Annobala's hair and dragged her to the dhekhal.

There was rain in the evening. After that like a young girl looking out from under her shawl, the full moon revealed itself in the sky. The wet leaves in the moonlight looked like golden fishes that jumped out of the pond. The puddles on the road had the colour of dry coconut shell. The leaves of the atlas tree, which looked like leaves of guava trees, and the leaves of ou, and jalfai trees looked like fluttering kanduli fish fished out of water. The clouds that reflected on the puddles opened up like the part of a huge umbrella.

Suddenly, there was the *ker-ker-gher-gher* sound of a bullock cart entering the Kakabori village. The cart stood outside the gate of Phuleshwari's house.

A man got down from the cart. Peering from the corner of the verandah where she stood, Phuleshwari saw an able-bodied man walk towards her. If it were not raining, Phuleshwari would have heard the *garap-garap* sound of the man's shoes. The clay lamp on her hand was lit dimly. It was the only light in the house. Hence, she was a little apprehensive to walk ahead with it. Yes, yes, look, the man was walking towards the verandah.

Seeing the man's face in the blended light of the clay lamp and the moonlight, Phuleshwari was surprised. The dhoti above his knees, a black coat, a very-visible cut mark on his forehead, it was the contractor, the Thikadar who came from Boitorani to hire labourers. Phuleshwari screamed, 'Why are you here?'

'Let me see, where is your ill daughter?'

'Why? Why do you want to see her? Have you brought some medicine?'

The Thikadar from the banks of Boitorani shook his head.

'For now, considering your hardship, I have brought a gunny sack of rice.'

'Rice?' It was as if Phuleshwari screamed. 'Do you have some tansak (ulterior motive)?'

'Ulterior motive?' Surprised, the man stood next to the dilapidated stairs of the verandah, as if he were not entirely prepared for such a question.

'What ulterior motive can there be? Your aapa is missing. Your aapi is ill. I have come to help.'

Phuleshwari said, 'Nobody has come to help us with a sack full of rice before.'

Yet, seeing the face of the Boitorani Thikadar in the shadowy light of the clay lamp, Phuleshwari was filled with wonder. Caught in the net of crisscrossing lines, his two eyes were like the eyes of an innocent man.

'You want to see Annobala? Come.'

Following Phuleshwari, the Boitorani Thikadar came

and stood near the dhekhal… In the thin light, the contractor noticed the woman who crouched in the corner. After a long look at the figure, he could not bear to look at it again.

Meanwhile, a labourer, huffing, with the sack on his back, stood next to the dhekhal.

A while later, the cart, with the *gher-gher* sound, left the way it came.

Holding the clay lamp, Phuleshwari stood there, not knowing what to do. Then, she mumbled, 'The dhekura wanted to spend the night. He left after seeing the girl. Otherwise, who would just give away a fat sack like this? Filled with rice, the sack looked like a pregnant cow. How can they be trusted?'

Carrying the clay lamp, Phuleshwari again went to the dhekhal. There, Annobala lay near a heap of rice husk, coiled like a snake. She could not gather the courage to carry the clay lamp any further. She backed out. The mekhela, which was tied to Annobala's bosom, now lay near her waist. She used the gatala as a pillow… The breasts of the young woman hung there like nests of bumblebees.

Returning, Phuleshwari sat on the verandah… There was the huge sack of rice. Will Annobala recover eating this rice?

Sitting next to the gunnysack, Phuleshwari started to howl.

***

Sitting on the dilapidated verandah, Phuleshwari, Bhubaneshwari, and even Annobala from the dhekhal, noticed that Choudhury's son these days would visit the widow Rajeswari. She was a daughter of Kakabori. Her husband died in a bomb blast on a bus in the North. It was surmised that the man was on the bus from a pair of shoes they found. She had some land in Kakabori. With the hope that she could sustain with the land, with the help of her brothers, she shifted back from the North to Kakabori.

...The people of Kakabori saw Choudhury's son Joiram carry the papers on his cycle to Guwahati, to fix Rajeswari's problems with the land.

Phuleshwari, Bhubaneshwari, and even Annobala from the dhekhal, noticed him going to Guwahati, carrying the papers on the back of his cycle.

***

Slowly, the rice from the gunnysack was depleting. One morning Phuleshwari and Bhubaneshwari stood in the courtyard of Kakabori's priest, Gaurikanta. Riddled with back pain, the priest lay on a bed. While performing a last rites ceremony in the house of a jajman in Moinabari, he was caught in the middle of a fight. It all started with a bed made of uriam wood that the dead man had left behind. From the fourth day itself, there was a conflict as to who would get the bed, the priest who performed the last rites or the priest who performed the main shradha ritual. Finally, there was an argument. In the melee, Gaurikanta Purohit tripped next to the bed made of uriam wood and fractured his back. The householders carried him back to Kakabori.

The Purohit's wife was a good woman. Yet, with householders becoming increasingly uninterested in organising religious ceremonies, even ignoring the annual ritual for their dead parents, and organising their weddings in Kamakhya Temple instead of in their houses, like other Brahmins in the locality, Gaurikanta Purohit was going through a bad patch.

Seeing Phuleshwari and Bhubaneshwari in the courtyard, the Purohit's wife screamed. 'Phuleshwari. You have stopped visiting us. Heard Anno's condition has worsened. Your boy hasn't returned yet…'

As she spoke, the Purohitani brought out a bamboo mat and spread it on the verandah. Mother and daughter both came up and sat on the verandah.

The Purohitani carried a bell metal plate of betel nut and leaves, and sitting next to the uriam wood post on the verandah, she started to dice the betel nut.

Then, suddenly, looking at Phuleshwari, she asked, 'Do you want me to grind it for you?'

Smiling, Phuleshwari said, 'No, no, aai, I have lost only a few teeth.'

'Yes, yes, Phuleshwari. I remember. You were the most beautiful woman in the whole village. After he married you from the north, Kinaram had come with a muga mekhela to seek blessings from us.'

Wiping the tears with her gatala, Phuleshwari said, 'With great hope, he brought me from the north.'

The Purohitani also heaved a sigh. Then, as she was about to say something about the inevitability of life and death, she stopped. Her eyes were on Bhubaneshwari. 'The girl is ready to keep her own japa. Will she be like this always? Don't you send her to school?'

Phuleshwari said, 'How do I send her to school? There are no clothes. Cannot run the household if she doesn't make the aeri threads. Beta, dhekura, after he grabbed the land, we three women have to spend the days with just one meal a day.'

The Purohitani was angry. 'You go there one day. Tell that bastard with no clan to have mercy on the girl and return the land. She has gone mad for him. You tell him, tell him, even if you have to lick his feet.'

The Purohitani got up and spat the huge red blob of betel nut sputum in the corner of the verandah. 'But, people from Kakabori say you allowed the girl to get mixed up with him.'

'Yes, aai, what else do you do? Young widow, she carried a rope on her hand. No saying what she would do next. I even tried giving her kani.'

The Purohitani screamed, 'You gave the girl kani?'

'Aai, there was no other way.'

The Purohitani again screamed, 'You begged before Joiram for opium?'

'He said other than him no one could get me kani. I begged that bastard with no clan.'

'What did he say?'

'He said there was no need to give her kani as yet. He said he would come one day and check on her.' Saying this, Phuleshwari stopped for a while. Then she started again, 'Aai, listen. One evening he came and stood next to the verandah. He said bring a bat lamp and hang it on the girl's room… Without knowing what to do, I kept the lamp on the jalia that hung in the room. He, beta, he kept staring at the aapi. Young girl, and filled with so much sadness… Her mekhela, gatala were all awry.'

The Purohitani screamed, 'Aai chikau! Why did the bastard with no clan enter the room of a woman like this?'

Hitting her forehead with the palm of her right hand several times, Phuleshwari added, 'Aai, I only destroyed my daughter by bringing him home, aai.'

Pressing her two eyes with the gatala, she started to weep intermittently.

The Purohitani, instead of trying to console her, poked at her and said, 'Chikau, in the room of a young girl… Whatever happened, happened. But, people say he went to Guwahati with the girl. Why did you let him?'

Phuleshwari again wiped her tears with the gatala. Then she inched towards the Purohitani, and whispered in her ears, 'In both north and south of the river, men with big bhakheris have started keeping two women. Nobody has raised issues. I thought Choudhury's aapa, who has three-four bhakheris, will keep her…'

The Purohitani screeched. 'Aai chikau, aai chikau, you, have you lost your marbles?'

Phuleshwari sat there in silence for a while... certain things hurt her heart like needles...

...I, Mrs Annobala Das, husband Dambarudhar Das, jati Hindu, profession farming, village Kakabori, thana Palashbari, mauja Sayani, district Kamrup, for the medical emergency of my mother, have kept one bigha land belonging to me as mortgage with Joiram for Rs 400...

'Uh, uh, the land was the only memento of her dead husband...'

This time, placing her head between her two knees, Phuleshwari started to howl,'...Bit me, bit me, he bit me on my very heart...'

This time, in a consolatory tone, the Purohitoni said, 'Come, Phuleshwari, come. Since you have come to clean the rice grains, I wouldn't disappoint you... If you see him on the road, hit him with your mekhela. Beta, I have heard he carries pills in the pocket of his patloon (trousers) to keep women from growing bellies. If the girl were pregnant, we could have dragged him to the panchayat.'

***

Carrying the small bundle of rice on her head when Phuleshwari and Bhubaneshwari returned home, the sun was showing its prowess above the chatiyan and chegun trees faraway.

On the Three-Road Chowk, they noticed a group of young boys who stood there surrounding the panchayat leader Harakanta and the Boitorani Thikadar. Phuleshwari knew the boys were from the families who lost their land in the flood. She stood next to them. Bhubaneshwari, however, ran towards the house. As she grew older, and as she did not have enough decent clothes to cover her, these days she would hide at the sight of any man. From the crowd, an old man cried out, 'Who knew our boys from the South will suffer this fate; will become soil digging coolies.'

Trying to keep calm, Harakanta said, 'Thikadar is here to offer a guarantee. The households whose boys will go with him will get money up to two kuris. He would not lead our boys to Kalapani. This money is the proof. We have seen this Boitorani Thikadar on the South side for the last two years.'

...Standing next to Harakanta, supporting himself with a stick, the gaobura said in a garbled voice with his toothless mouth, 'But, what kind of work will our boys do?'

Harakanta said, 'Will build a bridge across Boitorani River. Our Thikadar babu has received the contract to dig soil. They will get to eat and will get clothes to wear. While returning, he will give them the cash, no worries.'

The circle of the crowd had already become big. The boys who were going with the contractor ran towards the hill to collect whatever belongings they had. They were the ones who occupied the land that came under the Land Ceiling Act. Earlier, because the government paid no heed, there was no owner to the land. As the water claimed their land, these young boys from the wretched families were looking for hired land to cultivate. How would they get a chance so easily? The Boitorani contractor would offer cash—there was no bigger news than this in the area.

A while later, wading through the mob, Phuleshwari found Harakanta and the Thikadar on a bench under the pipal tree.

Pointing a finger at Harakanta, she said, 'Ask, ask Thikadar babu. Did he see my boy anywhere? It's been four years.'

Harakanta was irritable. 'He wouldn't return, your aapa wouldn't return. He has gone to the jungle.'

'What do I do? You know how the Choudhury's son grabbed the land from the girl.'

Harakanta was irascible. He was a big-bodied man. The flesh of his cheeks went up and down when he spoke.

'Why did you allow him to enter your house?'

In a soft, broken voice, Phuleshwari narrated. 'Young girl, that too, a widow, what could I do when he entered the house?' Suddenly, her voice became heavy. She screeched. 'Now, my girl is dying. How many people didn't I ask to help me free the land from his clutches! I cannot take the aapi for treatment in Guwahati. We three women are dying of hunger.' Saying this, and putting down the bundle from her head, Phuleshwari started to cry.

Harakanta said, 'Go, go, no need to cry in the meeting. Soon the boys will return to give their 'tip signatures' (thumb prints).

Meanwhile, the parents of the boys who had come to collect their shares of cash surrounded Harakanta and the Thikadar. Carrying the bundle of rice on her head, she returned home. For the entire stretch of the road, she walked carrying an unbearable pain inside her heart.

***

One night, all the three women woke up with a start. Walking straight from the embankment, crossing the forest of bamboos and chegun trees, three boys knocked on the door.

As Bhubaneshwari got up to open the door, Phuleshwari grabbed her hand. 'You look like a grown woman already. One girl is already spoilt; I wouldn't let you get spoilt.'

Pushing her aside, she opened the bar of the wooden door. In the dark, she could not recognise the men. One of them switched on a torchlight for a second. In that sudden light, she saw two tall and one short boys. They had guns in their hands.

Phuleshwari started to shiver.

They said, 'Hoibar is all right. Tell us if you have any problems. Keep the patta of the land that Choudhury's son has grabbed ready. We will come back for it. Tell us, do you need any money?'

Phuleshwari stood in silence. Then she screamed. 'Let Hoibar return. Let my own flesh return. You don't have to worry about us.' Sitting on the verandah in the middle of the night, she began to howl.

In a fraction of a second, the three gun-wielding creatures disappeared in the forest.

***

Finally, they were left with only the money Bhubaneshwari received from preparing the aeri threads. Working on it day and night, her fingers had bloated beyond recognition. Phuleshwari kept a tab on what was happening among her relatives and on the functions attended by the priests. Everywhere, she would ask anyone who cared to listen about Hoibar. She also narrated before everyone in detail the story of how the Choudhury's son grabbed the land. She also narrated how she could not offer Anno the proper treatment because of the loss of the land. Everyone made uh, ah, noises. They also suggested that she beat up Choudhury's son with a mekhela. But nobody dared to accompany her to Choudhury's house.

Why could not they drag the dhekura from his house and make him stand in front of Anno? Why could they not force him to make an arrangement for Anno's wellbeing?

...Sitting on the verandah, Phuleshwari was watching the japa thoba jowa procession of a young girl who had come of age. A strange scent from the bodies of the village girls assaulted her nostrils. The smell was the same smell of hyacinth and banana leaves that came floating on Dhaleshwari. Even from their clothes, which were boiled and washed and hand-pressed, wafted a scent like the scent of boiled old rice.

She noticed the girls clearly from her verandah. One had a huge hair bun. Another girl's skin was like the scales of a kokila fish. One was tall; another was short. The head of the aapi of the occasion was weighed down with the japa she was carrying on it, which was filled with betel nut, betel leaves, gamosa (handwoven towel) and scented flowers.

Their enchanting songs beckoned her to the past.

Japa-r xoru khati
Japa bandhey aati
A aai geet gai nagare chati
Japa-r murat ram chare
Urao urao kare
Baat dhekhu renu renu ghar kiman dur
Bulbake naru aami
Bharite lempur...

The japa has small sticks
The japa is shut tight
They sing spanning the whole town
On the japa's head is Ram
Ready to take off
We see the road faraway, how far is the house
We cannot even walk
We have lempur on our feet...

Her mind flew back to the past. When she had come of age, like all other girls from the upper side of the river, when she applied jamuki by burning a rod of lean bijuli bamboo and an iron knife on her teeth, what had happened to a tooth riddled with a cavity! She still remembered the pain. Still there was so much merriment.

The Ganak, counting the time and the stars, had said, 'You are saved, aapi, you are saved. If it were the third day, the season would have been unsuccessful. In the seventh day, beti, you'd have been a barren woman… On the tenth day, you'd have been a demoness, if it were amavasya (new moon night), you would have been plagued with diseases… on the other hand, if it were a Saturday, even being a menstruating woman you'd have been barren. This is the month of Aghon, that too the thirteenth day, such girls are pure. Like Chando Sadagar, you will be able to travel on boats.'

Everything was etched on Phuleshwari's mind like lines on a stone. Everything was sculpted in details on that stone…

There, before her eyes, Bhubaneshwari was growing up. What will she do? Will she be able to perform the procession of the japa? …No, no, she did not have anyone. Bhubaneshwari did not have anyone she could call a friend. She was always alone. She did not even talk to anyone. What would happen? Would she be able to perform the ritual? There was no money. If she begged, the Purohitani would give some!

Yes. Yes. Only the Purohitani understood her pain. Yet, even her condition was not good.

Now, there was another worry that settled on Phuleshwari's mind—Bhubaneshwari was increasingly becoming different from other girls, in her speech and behaviour. Sometimes in the looks of her eyes, Phuleshwari saw flickers of fire.

***

Bhubaneshwari came of age.

Meanwhile, there were situations three-four times when there was a need to take Annobala to Guwahati for treatment. Phuleshwari did not have any cash.

…Hiding her face between her knees, Bhubaneshwari was sitting near the bed.

There was a garment of paat hidden away for the occasion. (Annobala had purchased this dress with the money she received from the mortgage of the land. She went to Guwahati with Choudhury's son wearing this very dress. After she fell ill, she never bothered about the dress. Taking advantage of the opportunity, Phuleshwari had hidden away the clothes for the occasion.)

Knowing that the garment will be needed at the time of the ritual bath, when Phuleshwari reached for the wooden pera under the bed where the garment was stored, Bhubaneshwari screeched.

'Khabaddar, don't touch Anno's pera. You don't have to borrow money from the Purohitani to perform the bathing rituals. Khabaddar, I wouldn't allow any of this. If you try to force me, I will run away like Hoibar. I will also pick up a gun.'

Sitting on her knees in front of Bhubaneshwari, Phuleshwari began to quiver. What was she saying? What the girl was saying? Anno had come of age before her eyes. She did not behave like this. What was she saying? What was the aapi saying?

Phuleshwari was shaking all over. Then as if she was making a request, she said, 'What are you saying? Our condition is bad, that's true, even then we haven't come to such straits that we can't live in society anymore. Society is bigger than even our parents. Society and guru are bigger than our parents. We cannot survive without society. Didn't those people from the cowherd's village that the king banished from society became Musalman?'

For a long while Bhubaneshwari stared at her mother's face. Her mother noticed that slowly even her face was becoming cruel. The petals of her nostrils were flared. Her breathing was fast…

To pull the broken old wooden box, once again Phuleshwari crouched under the bed. Just then, the girl, who was menstruating for the first time, screamed, 'If you remove the garment from the box, I will leave the house right now.'

***

Sitting on the verandah, Phuleshwari kept weeping for a long time. She continued to mumble and curse herself. 'On whose food did I pour poison? She came of age in the morning, she will be barren… Girls who come of age in the month of Jeth become issueless widows… What other stars there would have been… If she came of age in Bharani, Rohini,

Adra planets, even the grass on the courtyard will turn to ash. Oh, oh, who will now count the days, stars, time… who? She came of age today morning and now, she is behaving like a warlike goddess.'

For a while she sat motionless. She remembered the words the Ganak said when Anno had come of age. 'The first day a girl comes of age, she is Chandalini. The second day Mahapaapi (a grave sinner), the third day, she is spoilt. She is free only on the fourth day. …Today, she is Chandalini… yes, yes, today, she is Chandalini… What will she do? Then what will she do?'

…When she was young, she had heard that in the fear that menstruating girls will not get husbands, in the families of Brahmins and Gohains, the girls were hidden away without anyone knowing. Spending four days on the cold mud floor of a room during the middle of winter, she had heard, once a Gohain's daughter on the South side of the river had passed away. In terror, Phuleshwari again started to tremble.

***

Meanwhile, the news that Bhubaneshwari was menstruating and that she refused to follow the prescribed rituals spread all around Kakabori. Finally, with the Purohitani's mediation and after she bowed before the gathering at the Naamghar, offering them betel nut and leaves, Phuleshwari was forgiven. At the time, what the Purohitani said was interesting.

Wearing a pair of riha-mekhela made of paat, standing amidst the crowd in the Naamghar, she said, 'Hasn't everyone on the South and the North side of the river now slackened their religious duties? Even Brahmins and Gohains have foregone their duties towards their ancestors. People know the state these three women are in. Still they have kept their eyes closed. The hell-worthy who grabbed Phuleshwari's elder daughter Anno's land, forcing her to go crazy, walk about in the village wearing canvas shoes and yet no one has done anything about it. Hoibar disappeared from this very Kakabori, could anyone do anything about it? Now, if she failed to follow the 'japa thowa parva,' what *Mahabharat* was destroyed?'

The series of arguments and counter arguments went on for hours. There were snarky comments aplenty and much hurling of abuses. Finally, everyone bowed before Purohitani's argument. It was the first time the Purohitani had attended a public meeting like this in the Naamghar. She was thin, and very fair. By now, her financial condition was so bad that she had to sell even the chador-mekhela the Purohit received from the householders. Yet, unlike other women in the village, she did not wear a gatala; she wore a chador.

For a long time, however, rootless boys of Kakabori never forgot to hoot if they saw Bhubaneshwari on the road. Sometimes, without warning, somebody would hurl hard lumps of soil on their courtyard.

No, no, she did not care about anything. She would carry the aeri threads she would prepare to the Marwari shop in the Three-Road Chowk and would return with long strides. It was her only job.

As if moving away from everyone else, Bhubaneshwari had cleared a road all for herself. She did not care about the arrows of the words on her ear and the hurt of the stones on her body.

***

Blowing the dust of the village one morning, an old ambassador car stopped outside Phuleshwari's house.

From naked boys to young girls to the elderly everyone surrounded the vehicle. One did not see such vehicles often in the village.

Four ladies got down from the car. Two of them were fat, elderly. They wore riha-mekhela of paat silk with cotton chador with borders. Their heads were covered with the end of the chador. The two young ladies wore muga mekhela with flowery patterns on it and cotton chadors with borders. Both of them were quite tall. One of them had short hair. She wore a pair of dark glasses.

Leaving her work, Bhubaneshwari came out of the house. Standing in front of so many people with her old and frayed mekhela-gatala, she looked uncertain.

The older lady with the covered head came forward and spoke. She spoke the language of Upper Assam. 'We were told a mentally disturbed woman lives here.'

Bhubaneshwari did not answer.

The mob, which was standing behind the lady pointed out, 'There is, there is, she is in the dhekhal.'

All of them surrounded the dilapidated dhekhal.

The two women who had covered their heads were perhaps from cultured families. They had never seen such a disturbing scene before. She lay there, next to an old duli used for collecting rice grains. ...Perhaps, a while ago, Bhubaneshwari had left some rice powder in a bowl along with a glass of black tea. The half-eaten rice powder was spread all over ...Did she also barf? All the women covered their noses with the corners of their chador. A foul smell pervaded the air.

Meanwhile, Phuleshwari came out of the house and hurriedly walked towards the mob. The ladies from the city said, 'We, the welfare committee, are now trying to offer free medical service to the ill. In the Three-Road Chowk, we heard that in Kakabori there is a patient. Hence, we came with the car to take the patient away.'

It was as if Phuleshwari and Bhubaneshwari found heaven within their grasp.

Phuleshwari sat on her knees before the women. Then, screaming, she narrated. 'It's been two years since she has been in this state. We could not take her to Guwahati. There is no money. The land in Mora Pora Bakara is in mortgage. Bhubaneshwari cuts the aeri thread to make money for salt and oil. Otherwise, the land I have in my name in Kakabori isn't enough to feed us for the whole year. Young son, Hoibar has disappeared. The metric-pass aapa, he went crazy looking for a job.' She started to wipe her tears with the corner of her gatala.

Now, one of the two women who had their heads covered asked, 'Since when has she been like this?'

After a short silence, Phuleshwari said, 'She has been like this since the land in the field where the dead are cremated was mortgaged.'

The women from the welfare committee asked in unison, 'With whom is it mortgaged? Why did you mortgage it?'

Phuleshwari again remained silent.

The women again asked, 'Why don't you tell us? With whom did you mortgage it?

The crowd that thronged the courtyard made a buzzing sound like bumblebees. Phuleshwari remained seated in the same posture.

Just then, Bhubaneshwari, who was never much of a talker, screamed, 'The Choudhury's son, Joiram dhekura, destroyed her. He seduced her to grab the land.'

The two sons of Joiram's uncle were among the mob. They yelped like beaten dogs. 'Oi, aapi, afflicted by the smoke of boiling rice, she herself went after him. She herself did the tip signature on the paper.'

Bhubaneshwari screamed. 'Everyone knows about beta haramzada (despicable man). Everyone knows he is pally with the piyadas (peons) and the taranis (clerks) of the court.'

'Instead of blaming your beti sister, you malign our dada… Beti, who wore blood-soaked clothes and did not purify herself, you…,' clenching their teeth, in anger, the young boys were about to hit her. However, as the ladies, with their heads covered, intervened, they could not reach Bhubaneshwari. There was a melee, with confusion all around.

Moving away from the crowd, putting her knees on her bosom, Phuleshwari started to wail.

Someone from the crowd said, 'Annobala's state is like cattle. On a sunny day, you drag her from the dhekhal to the courtyard and if it rains, you drag her back to the dhekhal…'

The naked boys and girls of Kakabori, who surrounded the car, started to giggle in merriment.

Bhubaneshwari said, 'When the land was not mortgaged, we could at least eat two times. Now, without money, we cannot take her to Guwahati for treatment.'

The elderly social worker approached Phuleshwari and said politely, 'We have seen the wretched condition through our own eyes. We live in Guwahati; it is just 20 miles from here.'

The two thin young beautiful women, who accompanied the old ladies, screamed, 'Now we will be late. We will also have to visit to village on the North side of the Brahmaputra River. We should now arrange for the girl to get into the car.'

The woman now bent down and whispered in Phuleshwari's ears. 'We are taking the girl to Guwahati for treatment. Our welfare committee will take care of the treatment and her wellbeing. You don't worry…'

Phuleshwari hurried inside and brought the garment she had washed for herself.

Who knew the skeleton-like Annobala had hidden so much strength within her! When the four women held her arms to get her into the fresh clothes, she shook them off. This could not deter the four social service women. On the North side of the Brahmaputra River, there were several patients like this. They were used to the procedure.

With renewed vigour, the two young women, fighting, dragged her out. The crowd in the courtyard clapped at the effort and parted. The scene became noisy.

'Move people, move. The madwoman goes to Guwahati. Move, move.'

Annobala screamed. 'Where do you take me, oi? Joiram promised to take me with him. Where is Joiram? O mother of my heart, where is Joiram?'

The youngsters who had gathered in the courtyard screamed in wild merriment. 'Go, beti, go to your in-laws.'

In a serious demeanor, the elderly woman tried to disperse the crowd who were clapping at the scene.

Finally, the discoloured Ambassador, blowing dust on the way, left the Kakabori road and reached the highway. The gang of naked boys, screaming and screeching, followed the car until the Three-Road Chowk.

Phuleshwari and Bhubaneshwari were also standing near the road. Once the car disappeared from their vision, they returned to the verandah and wept. Unusually, Bhubaneshwari was not a girl who cried. But today, after Annobala left, she sat next to her mother and wept for a long time.

Though they cooked the midday meal, they could hardly eat. In both their imaginations, they saw Annobala... She was recovering. Her untied hair, like the colour of a sticky kokila fish just taken out of water, was blowing in the wind. The scent of her clean mekhela and gatala, like the scent of the waters of the Dhaleshwari River during the flood, wafted in both their nostrils. Her clear laughter and her voices were heard everywhere.

Yes, yes, the doctors in Guwahati cured her completely. They finally were successful in recovering the land from Joiram's clutches. The victory of good over evil. Yes, yes. Good will prevail over evil.... It was as if heavy burdens were lifted from their heads.

As if after a long time, Phuleshwari and Bhubaneshwari had the time to lift their heads and look at the sky. Standing next to the well, both scanned the sky. It was a clear sky. Even in the sunlight, they noticed a piece of the faded moon, as if it was a silver-white boat submerged in blue water.

At night, embracing her daughter, Phuleshwari said, 'We are rescued of the spending on the girl. Since she has been taken to Guwahati, she will now be all right. All your clothes are torn. This time from the money you get from the aeri threads, you will be able to buy some new garments.'

Bhubaneshwari did not reply.

...Both of them kept their ears open. Perhaps the news of Annobala's leaving reached that mysterious place where Hoibar lived. Yes, yes. Perhaps the gun-wielding boys would come tonight for collection of land papers.

Both were thinking the same thing. Once they had the proof from the papers, they will shoot both Choudhury and his son. Killing. Mahapaap, Mahapaap. Sometimes both were numb with terror, as these days police vans were roaming around Kakabori, blowing their whistles. Ah, has someone noticed? ...These days, they had stopped talking about Hoibar...

***

Not even a month was over, and the colourless, old Ambassador again appeared in Kakabori and stood in front of Phuleshwari's house. ... Again there was a skirmish among the naked boys and girls of Kakabori. They surrounded the car smeared in a thick layer of dust.

This time, like earlier, the four women did not disembark. Two agile, middle-aged men in the khaki dress of watchmen alighted from the vehicle. Both shooed away the gathering children. Then they helped Annobala get down from the car.

Dear god, dear god, there was no change in the patient. She returned in the same pair of clothes in which she had left. Her hair was unkempt. The bones under her neck were visibly protruding.

...Holding her from both sides, the men in chokidar uniform sat her on the verandah. Sitting on the verandah for just a moment, like a snake slithering towards its hole, she ran to the dhekhal.

Surprised, Phuleshwari and Bhubaneshwari stood motionless on the verandah. On their faces were lines of astonishment. The two uniformed chokidar said, 'There was a big fight between the ladies from the welfare committee and the political leaders who had joined hands with the hospital authorities… This was the result. We had to transport all the patients back to their houses.'

***

A year rolled by. Annobala never recovered. With lack of treatment, she barely remained alive. As if in a dilapidated bamboo cage the lifelike bird fluttered to remain alive. …Sometimes, at midnight, keeping their ears to the ground, Phuleshwari and Bhubaneshari would sit on the verandah. True, perhaps they will hear the sound of Hoibar passing by.

…But no, for a long time, even the shadows of the boys who walked cautiously in the dead of the night were not visible. …Under the huge hollong tree in the middle of the village, suddenly a police chowkie came up. There was news that the boys from Kakabori and the banks of Dhaleshwari River had links with the terrorists who were settled in Garopahar. Blowing dust, even in the middle of the day, the police vans started patrolling the village. They even arrested a few boys from the village.

As Annobala struggled to remain alive in her sanctuary at the dhekhal, blowing dust one day the lorry of Boitorani

Thikadar descended. The contractor got down from the vehicle. ...A thick brush of mustache under his nose, clean dhoti, black half-coat, fountain pen in the pocket, thick boots on his feet... The colour of his skin was pitch-black. The hair on his legs was straight. As he wore the dhoti above his knees, it looked like his legs were smeared in oil. On his head was a cap made of black cloth. Famous as Boitorani Thikadar, no one knew the real name of the man. Looking at his attire and his health, no one could guess how old the man was. Though the looks of his small eyes were deep, nobody could guess, looking at his eyes, what he was thinking. The petals of his sharp nose sometimes fluttered in some thought which no one could fathom.

With confident strides, he walked up to the dhekhal. Round, Annobala was sleeping like a jalpahia snake. Her dirty hair, like a broken old pot, was beginning to clamp. There were spots on her fair skin as if they were wild mushrooms.

For some time, the contractor stood there in wonderment. Then, looking at Phuleshwari and Bhubaneshwari, who were standing on the verandah, he said, 'If you don't take her to Guwahati for treatment, she will die.'

Both remained silent.

Again, in an emotional voice, the Thikadar added, 'Looking at your condition, no one wants to lend you money for treatment. There is no hope that Hoibar will ever return.'

Phuleshwari responded helplessly.

'The land in Manuh Pora Bakara was everything to us. Selling the proceeds from the harvest of the land, we could have treated her. ...Biting right in our hearts, the Choudhury's son grabbed our land.'

Towards the end, her voice broke. In an unnatural tone, she started to curse Choudhury's son. 'Bhithi utha, you without a clan, you die...'

'The demon who drinks the blood of issueless widows, die, die...'

'Knocking on the earth, I curse you, die, die, die...'

Suddenly, a piece of small firewood hit Phuleshwari. All three turned in surprise. The half-dead woman in the dhekhal had thrown the stick. Where did Annobala find such strength? Where?

...All three stood there as if they were struck by thunder.

Now, making a sign with his eyes, the Boitorani Thikadar asked Bhubaneshwari to go to the thicket behind the house. Cautiously, she walked towards the dense bush filled with titachapa and hollong trees.

He followed. The dry leaves rustled under his footstep. Through the leaves of the trees, sunlight landed on the man's body in perfect spots. ...As if for a moment, the man was transformed into a cheetah. Boitorani Thikadar gawked at the girl, who stood supported by a hollong tree, like a blazing fire.

...The colour of her gatala was like an old, unused palengi fishnet. Boitorani Thikadar could not look at the sight for long. He said, 'You come with me. In one year's time, you will earn enough money to free your land.'

She asked, 'What work would I have to do?'

'I would not ask you to dig soil. You will help the cooks in the langar. ...Last time, we had taken several Assamese women from the North to water the concrete and to lift soil. They are still working for us.'

Helpless, Bhubaneshwari asked again, 'If I stay away for six-seven months, who will look after mother and sister?'

The Thikadar, who did not speak the dialect of the region fluently, spoke softly, 'You don't have to worry about it all that. Now, you all three look like flesh of a goat in an open field... Who knows who will end up finishing you... You just come... In six month's time, you will save some money... Then you will be able to think about the land.'

Without a second thought, Bhubaneshwari replied. 'I will come.'

***

Bhubaneshwari went to work with the Thikadar.

Phuleshwari remained to keep watch over Annobala. Even her own health was deteriorating.

People on the way to the haat (weekly market) would sometimes notice her alone in the dhekhal, cleaning rice.

The women on the way to fish would notice Annobala spread on the mud floor of the courtyard. Heaving sighs together, they would murmur, 'God, don't make anyone suffer the same fate.'

In Bhubaneshwari's absence, the naughty boys on the way from school would roam around the thicket behind the house. They already finished all the guavas in the tree, even before they could ripe. Sometimes they would haunt the dhekhal and throw around the ugha-chereki and other paraphernalia of the loom. They would draw lines on the walls of the dilapidated adobe house…

Right now, Phuleshwari's house in the middle of the village looked like a scarecrow in the middle of a vegetable patch.

At midnight, the neighbouring households would hear whimpering and the sound of her weeping. Like the *hook, hook* sound of the sahadeb bird, her weeping spread breaking the depth of the night. Nobody could ascertain who was crying, Phuleshwari or Annobala?

Hook! Hook! Hook!

Hook! Hook! Hook!

Sometimes Phuleshwari was seen sitting near the dhekhal. If someone asked, she would say her knees hurt. The hurt stemmed from continuous pumping of the dheki while cleaning rice.

Passersby made comments. 'The piece of land made all three of them crazy.'

Sometimes when they would see Annobala outside the dhekhal, they would drag her to the bed inside the hut. While leaving, they would admonish Phuleshwari. 'You'd die. Aapi, you'd die. You wouldn't have anyone to offer you water. Why did you have to send Bhubaneshwari away as a servant girl?'

The scenes of Phuleshwari doing everything alone, from lifting water from the well, to clearing the courtyard to cleaning rice from the husk was heart-wrenching. …And slowly, the villagers even got used to Phuleshwari sprouting heart-breaking curses intermittently. The entire village was poor, wretched. Who would help?

***

Two months passed. No one came with any information about Hoibar. Now, the sky was visible through the holes of her roof. A labourer from Kakabori, who also went with Boitorani Thikadar, returned home.

Standing in Phuleshwari's courtyard, he said, 'No need to worry, no need. She is working, turning her blood into sweat. She cooks at the langar both the times. Receives overtime. She is saving money, one kuri at a time. And Boitorani Thikadar. Beta, he guards her with a dao (machete). If someone asks about you, she cries.'

Phuleshwari wanted to ask the labourer more. With the gamosa she had on her shoulder, she wanted to clean the dust of his hair.

'Beta, he was guarding her with a dao. Remembering her, she weeps.'

Iss, iss, iss, iss, iss, iss, iss, iss!

An otherworldly light that reflected on her shrivelled face for a while erased the ugly lines on her face. …Ah, she was on her way to plant rice paddy on Annobala's field…

Hoibar had returned. He was now a strong-shouldered youth… Look, with the plough, he entered the field. …The gold rice grains were filled everywhere.

Meanwhile, several young boys, who had gone with the Thikadar returned as well. Standing in her courtyard, everyone narrated the same tale.

'Boitorani Thikadar is standing guard with a dao in his hand.'

'No worries.'

'No worries.'

…There will be cash. They will free the land.

Another two months passed. With the beginning of the month of Jeth, there was incessant rain like drumbeats. Phuleshwari's courtyard and the rear of her house were filled with vegetation. On the two papaya trees, the creepers of bhat kerala and bhol spread with such dense foliage that during the night the two trees looked like a wild elephant.

This jungle of German grass and bhatara had to be cleared before Bhubaneshwari arrived. Yes, yes, let her be surprised. Let her be surprised. Ah, let her be surprised.

After a spell of rain, the sun was back in the morning. In Jeth, when the sun came up after a long spell of rain, all the creepy-crawlies under the earth left their holes and came up. Phuleshwari had gone to the Choudhury's house in Moudubi to clean rice husks. While returning, on the threshold of the door, a gomm snake passed by her feet. Entering the dark hut, she could barely stop herself from slipping on the floor.

One day, one of the fishwives came and informed her, 'Somebody felled a bheleu tree near the bridge. The stump remains. If you don't go and cut the stump for firewood, it would be difficult for you to survive during the rains.'

Soon after the kind-hearted woman informed her so, Phuleshwari ran to the bridge. Though she had the experience of dicing firewood with an axe, today, it was as if her old body was somehow filled with vigorous strength.

She started to hit the tree stump with the axe. Breaking open the silence of the forest at midday, the sound of her axe pervaded the air.

Ghap! Ghap! Ghap!

Ghap! Ghap! Ghap!

The noonday sun started to beat down on the back of this 62-year-old woman. She had no time to bother about it.

Ghap! Ghap! Ghap!

Ghap! Ghap! Ghap!

There was just this sound.

Carrying the bundle of firewood on the head, huffing and puffing, she returned and dropped the bundle near the dhekhal. Then reaching Anno, who lay near the dheki, she started to shake all over. Anno lay on her face in a pool of vomit. ...Was she dead? Hurriedly, Phuleshwari picked up her head. No, she wasn't dead. She wasn't dead.

There was another spell of rain during the evening. First, when she heard the *dhop, dhop* sound of the falling raindrops, she thought they were the drops of rainwater which were on the leaves of the banyan tree outside the house. Soon the *dhop, dhop* sound turned into unbroken sheets of rainwater. Soaked in the water that fell from the holes of the thatched roof, Phuleshwari and Anno sat under the bed, coiled like two old vultures.

Hunger and the exhaustion resulting from the whole day's axing had made her half-dead. …Just then, she heard someone knock on the door. She screamed, 'What happened?'

There was another *dham, dham* sound on the door.

'Oh, what happened?'

Her fight to free her land was now known everywhere.

'Oh, what happened? Oh, what happened?'

Will Choudhury's men throttle her? Who knew? Who knew? In lust for land, it was said men turned into wolves. …Another eight months, another eight months… Bhubaneshwari will count each penny and bring home one and half thousand rupees. Land is Lakhi (Goddess Lakhsmi). Land is Lakhi. Land is Lakhi.

Dham! Dham! Dham!

Dham! Dham! Dham!

…As if someone was trying to break open the door. Slowly, haltingly, Phuleshwari got up. She felt a piercing pain in the joints of her hands and legs. Somehow, dragging herself, slowly she opened the door. She stood there like someone hit by a thunder. Outside, drenched to the core, there stood a woman.

Lifting the clay lamp with her quivering hand, she drew it towards the face of the other woman.

Yes. Yes. It was Bhubaneshwari.

The two men who accompanied her, urged Bhubaneshwari encouragingly. 'Go, go ahead.'

'She came drenched in rain all the way from the riverbank.'

Phuleshwari screamed, 'Who are you two?'

'We are the men of Boitorani Thikadar. We have returned. Bhubaneshwari came with us without telling anyone.' Saying this, they returned the way they had come.

It was as if the sound emerged breaking open her heart. 'Why did you return like this? Why did you return?'

Bhubaneshwari came inside. Together they forced shut the door, which the howling wind was trying to blow away, and barred it.

They sat on the bed, soaked in rainwater. Then they started to weep. Placing Bhubaneshwari's head on her bosom, for a long time, Phuleshwari howled and howled.

***

When the dawn broke after the rain, the sunlight was dull and the atmosphere was somewhat depressing. Even the birds were quiet this morning, except a few crows screaming ka, ka... As if the entire world had transformed into a large copper vessel. ...As if some sort of sadness was mixed with the light of this copper vessel.

Leaving the house, walking slowly and cautiously, trying not to fall in the slippery mud of the courtyard, Bhubaneshwari walked towards the well in the backyard.

In the last four months, the area surrounding the well had turned into another world. Look, German grass and wild creepers have covered everything. Iss, iss, amidst this forest, in the hut that looked like an anthill, her old mother lived for the last four months.

Crossing the courtyard filled with rainwater and slime, both, walking slowly and cautiously, reached the well. Both were horrified when they saw each other in the daylight. So far, they had seen each other just in the flickering light of the clay lamp. Now, when they saw each other in the light of the day, both were surprised. Look, the rough skin of the body was sagging. The short hair had turned all grey. That her eyes had cataract was visible even from far away…

Seeing Bhubaneshwari, Phuleshwari was speechless. She had lost weight. Even her demeanour was dull. On her hand, what was that mark? What mark?

After a bath, mother-daughter sat next to Annobala, who had already returned to her usual place in the dhekhal, and had black tea in glasses. Today, even Anno had tea like other people.

'Why did you return like this, without telling anyone?'

Bhubaneshwari could not devise an easy answer to her mother's question. In a swift movement, she got up and carried the tin box she had bought from Boitorani to the dhekhal. She opened the box in front of her mother and Annobala.

She opened a bundle wrapped in paper. All three women gawked at the currency notes. None of them had seen so many currency notes in their lives.

Repacking the notes, Bhubaneshwari said, 'This I have saved through hard work in the last four months. With this, we will be able to free at least half of the land from Joiram. After sometime, I will return to work again. Then we will free the rest of the land. I was worried about you…'

***

In the morning itself, the mother-daughter duo got ready to wage war to free the land. Both Phuleshwari and Bhubaneshwari had never set foot in Choudhury's house. On the way, they met the Purohit.

Bhubaneshwari was impatient. 'We have got things to do at home. Let's finish this fast.'

It was then the Purohit noticed Bhubaneshwari. 'Ah, aapi is back. She must have brought cash. You have come to free the land? …Beti, you forgot the priest after getting the cash. To save money, you did not even consult me on an auspicious day. …Ah, losing weight the girl has become like the dry berry thorn.

The way the Purohit spoke it was as if he would just fall on his face on the middle of the road. He was going through a severe financial crisis. To top it, his back still hurt.

As they stood in the middle of the village road, several women, who were of the same age as Phuleshwari, came out of their houses. They wore just the mekhela tied above their breasts. As they were busy with their morning household work, they did not have the gatala on them.

Seeing Bhubaneshwari, curious, they said, 'Now the old woman's hunger for the land will satiate. The Boitorani Thikadar came to you like a god.'

'... Aapi looks like a dry bone...'

'...Oi, Phule, Hoibar's party shot dead two Marwari mahajans. Our Mantepi's father on his way to court saw this through his own eyes. The dead bodies were on the road ... Nobody could catch them...'

Phuleshwari's heart started to flutter. She wished if she could go to one of these women's houses and have a glass of water.

...No, no, there was no time. If they delayed, Joiram might leave the house. Going to Guwahati and the kachari was his only job.

Leaving the busy Kakabori road, flaked on both sides by houses, they hurriedly reached the gate of Choudhury's house.

Joiram was sitting on a barpeera in the verandah. Sitting on a peera, his wife was grinding something. On a chalani (bamboo sieve) in front of her, there was some powder. They both could not ascertain what powder it was, halfali or xilikha?

Opening the bamboo gate, they entered the courtyard.

Fleshy Joiram's lithe wife removed the gatala that covered her head, and said, 'You came very early this morning?'

An air of irritation passed by Joiram's face as well. 'You bought the girl so early in the morning. Heard Boitorani Thikadar took her away to dig soil.'

Phuleshwari and Bhubaneshwari looked at each other. Meanwhile, Phuleshwari had sat down on the courtyard, with her head between her knees. These days she got tired easily. If she kept standing for a long time, her head started spinning.

Look, even Joiram too had changed a lot. He had lost most of his hair. Even the mustache under his nose had turned completely grey. He had put on even more weight than before. Even his brushy eyebrows were now black and white; his eyes were puffed up and red. Perhaps crossing the Dhaleshwari River on a boat last night, he had gone to Badulipara to see the Jatra performance. The party was from Bangorabari. All young boys from Kakabori crossed the river to enjoy the Bangorabari Jatra Party.

Widening his blood-shot eyes, Joiram said, 'You bought a bad name to Kakabori by sending the aapi with Boitorani Thikadar. Next month, I heard, even the daughters of Dhani Kaamar and Nanda Kaamar will go to dig soil. The Thikadar has tempted them by saying that private companies make a difference between men and women, but in his company, there is no such difference. Everyone gets the same money. Even the gaobura has tempted everyone saying that his accounts are good. Do you think I do not understand Boitorani Thikadar's bhelkibazi (magic)?

Phuleshwari did not let Joiram finish. She said, 'You know very well why I had to send the aapi away. Today she has performed her magic.'

'Bhelkibazi!' Bhubaneshwari, who stood a little distance away, said, 'I have not performed any magic. Why shouldn't the girls from Kakabori go out? I had to leave home to fight my hunger and to free the land from mortgage.'

Joiram and his wife could not have imagined that this small girl will be able to speak before them with such confidence. Both fell silent and stared at her. Then Bhubaneshwari did something amazing. Snatching the cloth-bag which was tied to her waist, and shaking it in front of them, she said, 'You took the land away exploiting my bai Annobala. I have brought back the money, counting each xhiki, adheli… Just five hundred is short in this bag. Today, we make a decision.'

As if Joiram could not believe his own eyes. He stopped on his track for some time and said, 'Why do you blabber like a woman possessed by a Bira (malevolent spirit)? Who says I exploited your bai. She was a barabhateri.'

Bhubaneshwari flared up. Pointing her finger towards Joiram, she said, 'If you utter another foul word against my sister, I will… I will…'

Phuleshwari grabbed Bhubaneshwari's hand and tried to force her to sit down. Following the commotion, the bonded labourers who worked for Choudhury, and the women who had come to clean the rice husks, gathered around the courtyard. Joiram's wife was lost; she did not know what to do… Though cunning like a fox, Joiram knew if he argued with the firebrand in front of him, she would not leave until he was naked.

Trying to ease the situation, he said, 'I have seen you before you started wearing gatala. Now, I see that Boitorani Thikadar has made you smart. Say whatever you have come to say.'

'We need the land. I have brought cash and coin, just five hundred short. This I can arrange in the next six months.'

Joiram said: 'Even after seeing everything, you speak with your eyes and ears closed. What profit have I earned from that piece of land in the last two-three years? It was drought for four-five years, then, there was the flood. What profit have I earned? You cannot just come here to free the land.'

...Phuleshwari and Bhubaneshwari stood there as if stricken by lightening. They felt as if they were sitting in front of a hungry tiger. It was useless to cry and pray and mollycoddle or threaten this tiger—every attempt was useless.

***

Bhubaneshwari's nostrils flared. Now, she realised she should have bought somebody with her who knew the laws. But her small, innocent heart could have never imagined that she would get entangled in a net like this. Gathering courage, she said, 'Keep this money and if not our land, clear some other land for us.'

Like a man enjoying a fine joke, Joiram laughed and said, 'Oi, Phuleshwari's daughter, Bhubaneshwari. This is all land. You are talking about patha (male) and khahii (castrated) goats.'

'Patha and khahii goats...'

'Yes, patha and khahii goats... You talk about land, but it's not like a patha and khahii goat that I can cut the leg, or the head or the intestines and give it to you...'

Seeing Joiram's cunning, everyone kept quiet.

Now, walking towards Joiram, Phuleshwari said in a pleading voice, 'Turning blood into sweat, aapi has collected some cash. How I have spent the last four months, people in the village know. Joiram, for you, how Annobala...' Her voice started to break.

Who did not know that Joiram was responsible for Annobala's condition? She wiped her tears with her gatala.

Once again, Joiram was worried that he would be stripped naked in front of everyone. He stood up. Then forcefully, he said, 'Why do you shed tears for the land? Did you not enjoy my money? Now, how can I just free the land? Did you not notice how much land the river gulped this year? Haven't I suffered loss by taking the land from you?'

Stopping her work of grinding medicinal fruits, his wife wanted to say something on behalf of the two women. But her fear for her husband was stronger than her empathy. She had not forgotten how she was beaten black and blue when she had once tried to offer her opinion.

This time, Joiram thundered. 'The accounts of the land have changed. I will have to consult the papers. But make sure you understand one thing. You cannot talk about the land for another six-seven years.'

With enormous patience, Bhubaneshwari was listening to him. Now, her patience wore off. She held her mother's shoulder and dragged her towards the gate, at the same time shouting, 'I will go to Guwahati. Even if I had to clean shit, I will go to Guwahati. Aren't there courts? You sucked Anno's life-blood away. This doesn't mean you will suck our blood too.'

The bonded labourers in the corner of the courtyard shifted uncomfortably.

'You are the aapi who drinks tiger's fat (a fearless and headstrong girl),' Joiram screamed from the verandah. 'Go, go, go to Guwahati. Haven't you seen the Jajman-Brahmins who were reduced to beggary—grass grew on their bones while they carried on with their cases, haven't you seen? You will suffer the same fate. The clerks and the middlemen will reduce you to beggars.'

Back on the village road, Phuleshwari had a feeling that she would just fall face down on the road. Holding on to Bhubaneshwari's shoulders, she could barely walk.

***

At midnight, though Phuleshwari lay on the bed, she could hardly sleep. She lay like this just to comfort Bhubaneshwari. Yet her ears were open. On the other hand, imagining that her mother was asleep, with her head between her knees, Bhubaneshwari wept for a long time. At midnight, they heard the sound of boots. Even snakes while entering their holes might make a sound, but the team of terrorists, when they stood at the kachu patch behind the house, they made hardly any sound. Not once but twice, Phuleshwari had seen two tall and one short boys, wearing the fatigues of a paltan and carrying guns, standing in the backyard. Today too, at the same time, they were here.

At the end of their tether, the two women kept their ears to the wall and sat alert. From the hole in the wall, they could see a piece of the moon in the sky, like a piece of a strong pillar. From the hole in the wall, it seemed as if the piece of the moon was determined to expose the picture of their insufferable pain.

Knock! Knock! Knock!

They might have received the news that she had returned to Kakabori. Yes, yes, they had come… What were they saying? What? They placed their ears to the wall. Someone whispered, but the voice was clear.

'That dhekura wouldn't return the land… Buri, today you confess, who is responsible for your condition? Tell us. …You will see him pay. On our papers, we have Boitorani Thikadar's name, speak, Bhubaneshwari, tell us yourself, didn't the Thikadar take advantage of you… Speak?'

They clearly heard the sound of Bhubaneshwari whine. Usually, Bhubaneshwari was not a girl who would cry easily.

But just for a fraction. Then again, the other side of the wall went completely silent, like a cremation ground at night… Suddenly, kicking on the wall again, they spoke again, 'Speak. We were told to hear from your own mouths.

That dhekura has destroyed all evidence. You two are the only witnesses. Speak. We don't have time. …We don't have time.'

Both inched towards each other. Bhubaneshwari placed her head on her mother's bosom.

Killing! Killing! Mahapaap! Mahapaap. No, no, even with pain of death, they will remain silent. In their hearts, they could not endorse this game of death played by the terrorists.

For a long time, with the knife of their accusations, they kept hitting the mother-daughter duo. They both bled, but did not utter a word.

The piece of the moon seen from the hole on the wall moved away. Yet, the two women did not utter a single word.

***

Suddenly, what hint did they get, with heavy footsteps they dispersed from the backyard… Phuleshwari heard one of them shout before leaving, 'Bhubaneshwari has become a beshya, a prostitute—she cannot speak. Cannot.'

They heard the sound of the boots of the paltans. It seemed, somewhere near, four or five paltans alighted from a vehicle, near the forest filled with hollong trees and tora creepers.

The boys who stood outside, hitting on the wall with anger and hatred, had actually fled.

***

Phuleshwari got up. Pointing her finger to Bhubaneshwari, she screamed, 'What did the boys say? Speak, what did the boys say?'

When Bhubaneshwari did not answer, Phuleshwari kicked her on her back with all her might and screamed, 'Bastard, beshya, they all tried to tear away my skin, yet I did not budge ...I treasured my honour in the knot of my anchol. Why did you become a fallen woman? Why did you suck my blood?

Though Bhubaneshwari did not answer, her nostrils flared. Her face reddened like someone near a blazing fire. She did not cry.

Now, in a swift movement, Phuleshwari got hold of Bhubaneshwari's hair and dragged her towards the door. As if the woman, within a matter of minutes, had acquired the strength of a demon. She started to hit Bhubaneshwari's head on the bar of the wooden door.

Annobala, who was sleeping in the next room making a *gher-gher* sound, crawled to the other room to witness the scene. Phuleshwari carried on. ...Finally she was exhausted. Blood began to flow from Bhubaneshwari's broken forehead. Now, stopping the beating, Phuleshwari started to cry, which was filled with intermittent whines.

It was midnight. Opening the door, Bhubaneshwari went to the well. Outside, the dull moonlight was like a stale barali fish. Making a rustling sound, two foxes fled from the nearby grove. The sound of the paltans' boots could be heard as far as the banks of the Dhaleshwari. In the heart of the night's darkness, the sound felt like the firing of gunshots towards the sky.

Standing next to the well, Bhubaneshwari peered down at the water below. A flicker of moonlight floated on the water. The top of the well looked like the face of a giant cannon. ... The sound of her mother's whining and the *gher-gher* sound of Annobala's throat hit the wall of her heart.

Bhubaneshwari lifted water from the well and washed the blood from her forehead. Then she splashed water on her eyes. Several times, she lifted water in the small lota tied with a rope to the dheki. To her, the *ker-ker* sound of the lota going down and coming up felt like someone biting on a leg of a pigeon with his teeth. As if someone was biting some invisible bones inside her. Once the blood was washed away, her forehead puffed up.

Standing on the verandah, her mother and Annobala were observing her shadow. The *gher-gher* sound was still in Annobala's throat. Saliva dripped from both the sides of her lips. ...Both were worried that Bhubaneshwari would jump into the well. If she died?...Finally, she returned.

Standing before Phuleshwari, setting aside her shame and fear, Bhubaneshwari said, 'These days, sarkar has made it easy for pregnant women to get rid of it. I know, I know. I don't even have to go to Guwahati. I can return a virgin just from the Three-Road Chowk. I know all about it. You don't consider me a simple aapi. I am not a simple girl.'

After a short silence, Bhubaneshwari screamed again, 'Listen. Boitorani Thikadar wouldn't come back to marry me. He is already a married man, with children. ...But I wouldn't clean my belly. Whatever it is, aapa or aapi, I will take care of it myself.'

Phuleshwari shouted, 'What would you say if they asked for the father's name? Bastard? I am saying, what would you say about the father's name?'

Returning to the verandah, and spitting a big blob of sputum, Bhubaneshwari said, 'I don't need the father's name. I don't care about anyone. I will stick to my word even if you skin me alive.'

***

There was nothing left in Phuleshwari's body. She fainted and fell to the ground.

There was a skirmish in the morning. There were sounds of boots everywhere. There was a lot of movement in the village. Did they catch someone?

Whom? Whom did they catch?

With Hoibar, three more young boys from the village had disappeared. Did they catch any one of them?

Dhap! Dhap! Dhap!

Dhap! Dhap! Dhap!

Ah. Was it the sound of gunfire?

Dhap! Dhap! Dhap!

Around this time, Bhubaneshwari went to the well again. In the light of the moon, her body throbbed like a fish caught in a net.

In the morning, a few people, including the Purohit, appeared in their courtyard. They called out to Bhubaneshwari.

'Come out, Bhubaneshwari, come out.'

She came.

Amidst the group of gun-wielding paltans, she noticed the priest with his dhoti above his knees. Inching towards her, the Purohit said, 'A dead body of a boy is lying near the bridge since last night. It may be Hoibar. Nobody is sure. Bullet wounds have disfigured the face. Go, you have a look, go. The military has found the body. He was killed by his own men.'

Pushing past the crowd, Phuleshwari and Bhubaneshwari stood next to the bridge. Now, moving from the dead body, everyone's eyes were on them. From among the crowd, somebody screamed, 'Did Hoibar come last night?'

'Last night?'

'Last night?'

Mother-daughter both went close to the dead body and peered at it.

Someone again screamed, 'Don't, don't go so close, the police had drawn the line.'

It was the same colour, the same limbs, yet it was not Hoibar. Hoibar's hair was not so dense. Beside the hair and a part of the forehead, everything else of the face had turned to pulp.

Ah, the hands and legs were the same. Even the colour of the body was the same…

Sitting on her knees next to the dead body, Phuleshwari started to cry. She said, 'This isn't Hoibar. No.'

From the crowd, a few of them screamed, 'Hey, silly woman, why do you cry? This is not your aapa Hoibar ...It's not the Hoibar you carried in your womb... You are saved, you are saved, then why do you cry...'

Phuleshwari got up. Holding Bhubaneshwari's hand, she walked away. She kept weeping all the way. 'The shape of the hands and the legs were the same, same as him....The jewel of whose heart was he? Why did it come to this? ... Bhubaneshwari, I cannot recognise these people anymore.'

Bhubaneshwari enwrapped her mother in a hug.

'Bhubaneshwari, I do not recognise anyone anymore. Not even you. I don't even recognise you, Bhubaneshwari. Bhubaneshwari! Whose heart's jewel was he? Why did he die like this? Why?'

Bhubaneshwari could not stand it anymore. She screamed, 'It was Hoibar.'

'Hoibar!'

'Yes. It was Hoibar. I recognised him. Everyone in the village recognised him. It was Hoibar.'

***

First published as '*Bhikhar Patra Bhangi*' in the collection *Tej Aru Dhulire Dhusarito Pristha* (Pages Stained with Blood and Dust), 1994.

The Blood of Devipeeth

Chapter One

ONE

The year was 1930. On the foothills of the Kamakhya Dham lived Aghor Dev Bhagawati with his family.

It was the rainy season. On the giant boulders on the way up to Devipeeth, there were thick layers of moss. When the sun came up after the rain, they looked like half-peeled shingari fruit. Youngsters on the way to Devipeeth would try to climb the boulders and slip. There were several roads upwards to the hill, but the children did not care about them. They liked this road filled with bhatara, thorny bushes and jetuli poka.

Opening the window, Padmapriya could see the pilgrims climbing up. Look at the party. They must have arrived from Koch Behar. The sound of their chatter and the rustle of their clothes could be heard from faraway. There were three old men and two old women. There were two kids. The kids were healthy. Whenever they ran towards the boulders, the elderly would scream. But the kids were not bothered by the screams. They kept pushing forward. Everyone in the group of the elderly walked with a stoop, as if they were a bunch of hargila birds, walking haltingly.

Once the party vanished from sight, Padmapriya noticed, from her window, a pair of newlyweds walk up the road towards the temple. The vermilion mark on the bride's forehead shone from afar, as if someone had boiled the red sun and turned it into a line on the woman's head. Next to a boulder on the way, look, the groom was trying to hold her hand. Intimidated, she was trying to hide her hands inside her clothes. She stopped herself from slipping by holding onto a bush. Looking at the mekhela with flowery patterns on it and chador made of paat silk, Padmapriya surmised that the bride was the daughter-in-law of some important officer from up North. It did not look like she was from Koch Behar or Gaur. The high-caste women from those places wore saris with red borders. On their feet, they drew lines of alta.

Suddenly, a cranky voice surprised her. 'What do you keep looking at through the window? Do some work. Do some work!'

Alert at the voice of her father, she left the room in a huff and came outside. Slowly, she had come to realise that on her father's voice nowadays, there was a smell of irritation. The empathy she received after the Shastri family left her here, that empathy was long gone. Now, she was becoming a burden on her family. She knew it.

Padma noticed that the two men who had come to consult horoscopes with her father were standing outside his prayer room. Both were old Jajman (patrons). Both wore dhotis. One of them was old. He wore his dhoti loose and tucked the end of the garment in the pocket of his blue shirt. He wore his hair with a distinct parting on the middle of his head and combed his hair closely. The other man was short. He was young, really a teenager. Even he had a parting in the middle of his head, but he did not comb his hair closely.

Hurriedly, Padmapriya carried two murhas from the courtyard and placed them in front of the visitors. Taking a murha from her, the older man asked politely, 'Aai, weren't you the daughter-in-law of Rauta? Hari, Hari, we heard that the Shastri family left you here…'

After a brief silence, he said again, 'What can you do? Everything is destiny. We heard that the man has already brought home a girl from Bongora…'

The short, stocky youngster with a reddened cheek added, 'This is injustice. These days, in many countries, people have stood up for causes like this. One cannot just sit there doing nothing. If needs be, one must even go to the court.'

'Court?'

Padmapriya did not wait anymore. She ran towards her room and, once inside, bolted the door. Yes, everyone had heard the news. People near the temple of the Goddess, people in far off places—everyone had heard the news.

She again picked up the small mirror that hung on the wall. She removed the blouse she was wearing. She even removed the chemise made of markin cloth that came to her knees and placed it on the bed. Then she bent down on her knees and tried to look at the small mark on her back. It was difficult. It was difficult! She could not look at it properly. Forcing her to undress completely, her mother had looked at the mark and screamed, 'Oh, oh, is this the "dhabla" mark? He left you just for this mark?'

Holding their umbrellas, a pair of middle-aged men was climbing up. Behind them was the stocky dwarf of Kamakhya Dham, Seng. He was busy leading the Jajman to the Kamakhya temple on top of the hill. Iss, his hands slipped from his back. He walked with a limp, like someone with just one leg.

Again, her hands went up to her back. Again, her hands searched for the smooth skin on her back. Was this spot on her back really so smooth? The place where resided the white spot! Was it really smooth?

It was an inexplicable feeling. Her throat was parched. Until now, several of her blouses had torn. Now, the way her hands found the way to her back, it had become a habit. That polished spot? Sometimes she would start scratching the spot with her fingernails. Blood sprouted from her skin, scarlet blood!

The shut window was ajar again. The dark boulders on the Mekhela Ujowa Road looked darker now. ...Yes, those were the headless bodies of the buffaloes sacrificed at the temple.

***

Again, Padmapriya was startled by the cranky scream. 'What do you do? What do you do? Why do you spend your days in the dark room? I have finished my puja. You come out.'

She hurriedly left the room and came outside. The pair of men who had come to consult horoscopes were sitting on the same spot. The smoke of the incense sticks covered the room. In the smoke, the two men looked like two statues made of copper.

Her mother screamed again, 'Take, take these glasses to the Jajman. Why do you stand there like someone hit by thunder?'

Padma placed the three copper glasses on a plate. Bending down on her knees, with polite decorum, she placed the glasses in front of the Jajman. Keeping the plate aside when she was about to get up, she noticed the two pairs of eyes on her, as if, she stood in front of them naked. As if, by peeking, they were trying to figure out where on her body was that white spot… Yes, yes, they wanted to see the white spot.

Until now, Padmapriya would run away whenever she would come across such a look. Today, however, she did not budge. Even then, one of them asked in a sly tone, 'What do you do all day?'

What do you do?

Just one sentence, and always, it turned into a stone, crashed on her and broke into million pieces.

What do you do?

What do you do?

...Before the wedding, Padma and the Doloi's daughter Lavanya would laugh and say, 'Decorate the plaits of your hair with flowers now. Later, you wouldn't have the time.'

'Ha, ha... These men, I have heard, munching on the body turns it into sugarcane pulp. After that, a woman becomes a sugarcane fibre caught in the cavity of the teeth.'

Both had hearty laughs.

Lavanya had said again, 'I have heard that it's a big household. Your days would be spent taking care of the elder brother's kids.'

'Ha, ha... Even in the middle of work, he would come and pluck flowers from your plaits. Will he allow you to return home during Vasanti Puja, Madan Chaturali, Shatha Barat? Ha, ha...'

Again, they had hearty laughs. Ah, all this was a long time ago. Forget gutimali flowers on her plaits; she had not even made garlands of gutimali for the Goddesses Chinnamasta and Dhumavati above the hill.

Then, it was as if somebody whispered into her ears. 'You haven't offered garlands of gutimali to Goddess Chinnamasta?'

'You haven't offered garlands of gutimali to Goddess Chinnamasta.'

'Ha, ha, ha...'

Padmapriya was spooked. Standing close to the window, the dwarf Seng was screaming, 'Move, move, move...'

Padmapriya wanted to close the window. But Seng did not budge. Showing his large, yellowed teeth, he laughed a throaty laugh. She noticed that his head was disproportionately larger than his body. The head full of hair was unkempt. On his body was a torn, frayed shirt and a baggy pair of half-pants. She averted her gaze.

Picking up the tray of areca nut and betel leaves, she again approached the visitors. Another Jajman, meanwhile, had joined them. They started a noisy argument about court-kachari.

'We have to fight. We have to fight. They dumped the married girl in the courtyard and left and we just sat there putting our heads between our knees.'

'Destiny. Destiny...' Beating his forehead with his own hand, Aghor Dev Bhagawati cursed himself.

As she entered the room, they all became self-conscious. Yet, the new Jajman with closely combed hair, who chewed on betel nuts incessantly, who was fixing the planets on the horoscope, lowered his round spectacles to his nose and said, 'This Hindu law has thundered down on our women. Didn't you hear how a Gohani from Rani Baha was reduced to a beggar on the street after she was deprived of her share of land? Now, throwing the burden of a married daughter on your head, they are making you dance like a wooden goose.'

Lifting his hands towards the sky, Bhagawati screamed, 'Standing in my courtyard, they spat on my face. They said I duped them. Coming from "Pargana", they threatened me in my very house. ...I duped them. I offered them a sick aapi.'

Then Padmapriya noticed that her father was running towards her. Before he could reach, her mother appeared from the dhekhal and stood in front of him.

Bhagawati screamed, 'I want to see my aapi's back. …I want to see this sickness. Let people see. Let everyone see.'

Her mother pushed her inside with her left hand. She was about to fall flat on the ground; she found the pillar on the verandah in the nick of time.

The three uncertain Jajman now told Bhagawati, 'You yourself will have to establish the pillar of dharma. It won't do if you get nervous like this.'

After the Jajman left, the entire house was wrapped in silence, like a cremation ground.

Again, Padma took shelter in the dark room. Pushing her hand inside her blouse, she started to smoothen the white spot. Just for a fraction of time.

Opening the window, she saw the three Gram Sevikas (young women volunteers during the freedom struggle movement) climb up towards the temple. They wore white garments, blindingly white garments, as if they were three sthalapadma (changeable rose) flowers, walking towards the temple of the Goddess.

***

The three Gram Sevikas came for a visit in the afternoon. They carried the blessing of Bapu (Mahatma Gandhi). While leaving, they left some books and some yarn. She had spun some yarn in front of them. Patting her back, they said, 'You know how to spin the yarn beautifully. Those who can spin the yarn like this, they can earn their own livelihood.' While leaving, they even cleaned the glasses, in which they had tea, with durba grass and manimuni saak, pulled from near the well, to make them sparkle.

She was about to have her siesta when there was a knock on the door.

'Who? Who?' She screamed.

'I am Lavanya.'

...She got up with a start and opened the door in one swift movement. Lavanya and she were childhood friends. While the other neighbourhood girls now hesitated to hold her hand or hug her, Lavanya did not have such misgivings. She gave Padma a hug and said, 'You will be surprised at what I am going to tell you.'

'Surprised!'

Yes, yes, you will be surprised.'

'What is left for me to be surprised about anymore? What is left? Everything is over. Everything is over...'

Lavanya embraced her again. Teardrops fell from her eyes. She said in a broken voice, 'Even if you are hurt, I must inform you. Bhubaneshwar will be coming for my sister Kamala's wedding. The new girl also might come.'

'The new girl?'

Padma understood. She lowered her head. Lavanya looked at her face and kept quiet for a while. Then leaning on Padma, she lifted her legs onto the bed and sat comfortably. A soft scent wafted before Padma's nostrils. She was lost for a while in the scent emanating from the body of the newlywed woman. As if it was the balmy smell of a freshly sliced dimaru. Something inside her heart crumbled.

Lavanya said again, 'Listen, you will have to confront Bhubaneshwar. I have come prepared.'

Padma stared at her without a blink.

Lifting her head, Lavanya looked at the door. There was no one at the door. People of this household did not suspect her. 'You cannot rot like this. They treated you like garbage and dumped you here. He may not even have seen you properly.'

'Meaning?'

'Meaning your limbs... and your bosom that rises and falls like waves. Most men are like wolves. If someone ever gets the taste of your flesh, he will be like a man-eater. You know, a man-eater chews and devours even the blood-soaked clothes of his kill. Human blood has this intoxicating taste. Even human beings love eating human beings the most,' Lavanya said.

'Sih, sih, sih... you speak shamelessly,' Padma admonished her.

Lavanya added, 'Now I understand a lot of things. Now I understand how a man's mind works.'

...The wooden window flung open in the wind coming from the Brahmaputra River. There was a couple, a bride and bridegroom walking towards the temple. Carrying an empty dola (palanquin), the two palanquin bearers were walking ahead of them. The bride wasn't on the dola. Perhaps she did not want to visit the Goddess on a dola. She took each step cautiously. Her head was completely covered. The paat silk garment on her body sparkled like froth on the Brahmaputra during flood.

Who was that behind them? A huge head. Unkempt hair. A gamosa on his waist. Yes, it was the dwarf Seng. Whenever he saw rich pilgrims, the dwarf Seng followed them. If needed, he also helped pull the goats brought by the pilgrims for sacrifice at the temple.

Lavanya made fun of him, '*Oi Bawna Seng, dibo pathar theng* (oi dwarf Seng, I will give you the leg of the goat).'

The bride, the bridegroom, everyone peered down at the window. Seng mumbled something under his breath. Nobody understood him. The hair on his head was straight. His face was filled with pock marks. The colour of his skin was like copper.

'Listen, Padma bengi, you can get a lot of things done by Seng. Do you understand?'

Padma looked at Lavanya.

'Have you understood?'

'I have.'

...After giving Padma the date and time of the impending wedding, Lavanya took her leave. For a long time, Padma held onto Lavanya's hands. ...Lavanya saw that her hands were shaking. Even a vein on her forehead was protruding.

...After a while, the vein turned into a trident. ...The vein on her forehead turned into a trident.

TWO

'...Very nice. Very nice. The garden looks very soothing...'

Padma was clearing the roots of the flowering plants with a spade. After offering her these words of encouragement, while standing nearby, her mother went to the kitchen.

...The dwarf Seng was breaking the lumps of soil with his bare hands. Lavanya knew how to handle him and she had taught all the tricks to Padma. She filled his pockets with the batasa (discs of boiled sugar syrup) and the coconut larus (balls) that her father's Jajman left for her father to offer during puja. He was cleaning the soil with his bare hands. Compared to his large head, his small hands looked like they moved faster.

His father worked as a helper in supplying wood to the crematorium at Kamakhya Dham. His mother had died soon after his birth. Nobody knew who started calling him Seng. Probably, it was some wily men from the temple. He received his sustenance from the temple.

The scent of incense wafted from her father's puja room. A pair of Jajman from the North had arrived early in the morning, to perform Shani Puja (rituals in honour of the Son of Surya, the Sun God; the God who removes evil and obstacles). The sound of her father's baritone chanting the mantras spread everywhere.

Shanayshwara mahabhaga lokanu grahakarak
Mool shakti samudvata namaste suryasambha
Namaste shoolahastiya palahastiya dhammine...

Then, standing next to her mother, Padma said, 'I have heard that there are saplings of white flowers on the west of Bhubaneshwari. …I'll go and take a look.'

'Go, go, aai. Take Seng with you.'

Her mother approved her plan enthusiastically. Truth to be told, for the last two years since her father-in-law left her here, she had hardly shown any interest in doing anything.

Standing near the threshold, her mother looked at Padmapriya. What a beauty! Not a single girl from Kamakhya could compete with her in beauty. Yet? Yet? She pressed her eyes with the corner of her chador. Then, why did this happen? Why?

***

With Seng, she descended from Bhubaneshwari. Both of them reached the plain where blossomed the saplings of white gutimali flowers.

Seng did not want to be there. He was desperate to leave. He was terrified to be in this haunted forest alone.

But Padmapriya? Holding his hand, she walked ahead. She did not have any fear. There was a scent of wild flowers everywhere. On the large stones on the banks of the Brahmaputra River, she noticed was a flock of egrets.

Padmapriya was trying to pull out a sapling with its roots. It was part of a bigger gutimali plant. As she and Seng, using all their hands, tried to uproot the plant, it suddenly came undone and the force caused her to fall onto a man who was walking by.

'Iss, iss, iss, whose daughter! Whose daughter!' Making a clamour, Shambhudev, the deo who performed the sacrificial rites, spent a long time looking for his kharag, his sacrificial sword, and the robab tenga, which fell from his hand during the impact. Seng followed the robab tenga, which was rolling down towards the river, jumped on it to catch it, and making a *bham, bham* sound with his mouth, returned it to Shambhudev.

Only after he had found his kharag, did he look into the eyes of the girl. He could not believe his eyes.

There was none as beautiful in Devipeeth as she was.

Who? Who was she?

Revealing his large teeth, Seng made a smiling gesture and pointed his hand towards Padmapriya's house.

For some time, Shambhudev stood there witlessly.

Yes. Yes. Now, everything was clear. Now he remembered. He saw the girl once or twice near the sacrificial enclosure. Then nothing. ...That girl, that full-bodied girl, just passed by him. He had never seen her like this before. It were, as if, there was a new body on her old flesh. The girl who stood next to the sacrificial enclosure and cried during the sacrifice had turned into another girl. Wondrous! Wondrous!!

THREE

One week later, carrying a khanti (hand spade) and a katari (curved knife), with Seng in tow, she again started out in search of flowers.

In the afternoon, after lunch, munching on betel nuts and leaves, when other people took refuge on their beds, she, with Seng, started their journey to the river. Bhagawati asked his wife sleepily, 'Has she gone somewhere?'

'Perhaps she has gone with Seng to look for white flowers.'

'White flower?'

'Haven't you seen how she has filled the garden with white flowers?'

'White flower?'

***

Surprisingly, on the second day too, Padmapriya noticed the bali kata deo (the priest who performs the animal sacrifice) Shambhudev near the river. Using his kharag, he would push a robab tenga from the gunnysack to the water and then, with his sacrificial sword, he would slice the floating fruit into two with a single blow.

With great curiosity, Padma and Seng observed the scene. Shambhudev was full of muscles. The veins of his hands and legs were protruding. On his entire body, there was a visible manifestation of masculinity; his shoulders were like a lion's, his arms like iron. It was as if, the blood flowing under his calf was visible from the distance.

Failing to sustain her curiosity, Padmapriya screamed, 'Bali kata deo, what are you doing? What are you doing?'

Shambhudev turned. The kharag fell from his hands.

Involuntarily, he started to chant: '*Om, louha dattaye namah. Om, lauha dattaye namah.*'

Shambhudev Shikdar picked up the fallen kharag. 'Why do you come to this haunted place at midday?'

She and Seng did not answer.

'Why do you come?'

'Bali kata deo? What is this talim (practice)?'

'Redemption. Yesterday, during the buffalo sacrifice, it took me three blows. I am doing talim so that this does not happen again.'

All three remained quiet.

'Besides following the redemption rituals prescribed by Devipeeth, I want to come clean, in every which way.'

Keeping the scimitar next to a rock, Shambhudev walked up from the water. From the river, there wafted a smell like the smell of raw meat. It was the month of Bohag. Perhaps some hills had fallen on Brahmaputra in the flood. It was a mixed smell of damp clay and tree roots.

Holding onto Seng, Padmapriya sat on her knees. 'How many buffaloes have you sacrificed so far…?'

Shambhudev looked at her face for a long time. Then he said, 'Three thousand buffaloes.'

'Three thousand buffaloes?' Padmapriya screamed.

'Today morning, it took me three blows on the buffalo that the Mahajan (trader), paralyzed with fear from his enemies, had offered…'

People from the Garo village were sitting on the stairs of the Good Luck Pond since morning. They had heard the news.

Mumbling to himself, the giant man with lion's shoulders, looked towards the sky, and said, 'I recited the bakkhyaman mantra...'

In his mind, he started chanting the mantra.

Yatha vahang bhabana dwesthi yatha
Rahasi Chandikam
Tatha mama ripunag hingsha shubhang
Waha lulapakasamashya vahanastunthu
bararapasharabyaya
Aturbitong yasho dehi kashyabaya
Namo hante te...

Oh Mahish (buffalo), the way you carry Chandika on your back, you defeat my enemies. Bless me.

The buffalo was decapitated to fulfil the wish to defeat his enemies. The enemies were invoked in the sacrifice. Oh, yet, it took three blows. Ah, Devi. Ah, Mahamaya.

'The people from the Garo village are now cleaning the kill under the banyan tree. Go, go, and see. They are carrying the meat home.'

For a while, Padmapriya and Seng remained silent.

'Deo, does Devi accept human sacrifice too. Does she drink human blood?'

'Human sacrifice? It's in the scriptures. If a human is sacrificed with all the prescribed rules and rituals, the Goddess is satisfied for a thousand years. With three human sacrifices, one lakh years... with human flesh, the goddess is satisfied with three thousand years. …Listen, to understand the right way to pronounce the mantra to offer oblation to the sacrificial sword, I have toiled for many years…' Saying this, he again tossed a robab tenga to the water and then sliced the floating fruit with the kharag.

This was the rehearsal for a sacrifice. This was a rehearsal not to waste a sacrifice.

Holding Seng's hand, she walked ahead through the small track, and crossing the pama, muni and uriam trees and thorny bushes, they stopped under a giant amlakhi tree. Here, the creepers on the trees were hanging so low that the leaves entangled with her hair bun. On the way, bees from a honeycomb somewhere flew in and sat on her forehead. Elsewhere, she had to skip and jump over the stones that looked like the Goddess's feet, as devotees had smeared them with sindoor and covered them with garlands of tulsi leaves. …Yes, it was possible that she could step into the dismembered body of the Goddess, which was perhaps destroyed by Kalapahar. Finally, they reached the old banyan tree and stood under it.

The people from the Garo village had already cleaned the buffalo and now, they were all set to carry the meat back to their village. Look, how the blood splattered all over the grass. Look, there is one discarded hoof. Padmapriya remembered. Oh, when the buffalo was hauled to this place, how it found it difficult to climb the stairs. Oh, oh, how fearfully it looked everywhere. Look, the dismembered flesh of its body now lay scattered in front of her.

Oh! Oh! Oh!

What happened? What happened to her? Falling down on her knees, she started to cry. The dwarf Seng jumped around her and started to whimper. Look, now Shambhudev, instead of slicing the robab tengas, was looking at her.

***

For two days, she did not climb up searching for white flowers. She bolted the doors and stayed inside the dark room. ...Intermittently, she would try to stand in front of the mirror and inspect the white spot on her back. She would not see anything clearly in the dark room. Yet, she would continue to struggle. No, no, the spot remained the same. It did not increase. It did not disappear. As usual, she first started to smoothen her back. Then, she started to scratch it. ...Then, in pain, she lay on the bed.

FOUR

One week later, Lavanya came down with two girls. Seeing the girls, Padma's mother Yashobai was very happy. All these days, Padma had been hiding in the dark room. Meeting the two young daughters of the panda (priest), Padma would be happy. Sure, she would be happy.

'Go, go, she is inside.'

While Lavanya immediately went inside, the two girls stood there, uncertain and apprehensive.

'Why don't you go inside the room?'

No. They did not answer. Now, Yashobai shouted as if she was admonishing the girls. 'Go, go, she would be happy to have company...'

Yet, the two girls remained uncertain.

Now, Yashobai started to scream. 'Idiots, you have come to enjoy the show. You think my daughter has white leprosy... That's why those dogs left her here... Idiots, idiots, look, look, look through your own eyes.'

Saying this, like a woman possessed, she went inside and dragged Padmapriya out. There was a scrimmage. When she tried to rip Padmapriya's blouse, to reveal the white spot, Bhagawati, who was sitting with his Jajman, reprimanded her, 'What are you doing? What are you doing?' Only when he held his wife's hands did she stop.

The girls who had come with Lavanya, ran away to their houses up on the hill. Lavanya stood there not knowing what to do. Her heart cried out. 'Yes, yes. Things were like this. Things were just like this...'

...After a while, huffing and whimpering, Padmapriya went back to her room and sat on the cot. Lavanya wanted to go and hug her, but today, now, she could not do it. Sitting on a peera on the verandah, Yashobai was beating her chest. Then she started to curse the Shastri family with the choicest of words.

'Die, die, you all die. Let your clan be extinct. Let it be extinct.'

...Bhagawati stood next to her and shouted, 'Jajman is here. You shut up. Shut up. Your tongue has lost its control.'

While leaving, Lavanya whispered in Padmapriya's ears, 'Just 20 days are left for the wedding. Remember, just 20 days. I have heard that the Brahmin's daughter from Koch Behar has failed to give him an offspring yet. Two years have passed. I have heard that the man is irritable, with withered limbs.'

***

Waking up in the morning, Padma saw Seng stand near the dark stone like the belly of an elephant, near the Mekhela Ujowa Road. In his hand was a bunch of white kunda flowers. He was looking at the tiny wooden window of her dark room. Showing her the flowers, as if, he was trying to tell her something. What? What was he trying to say?

Several parties of pilgrims passed through the Mekhela Ujowa Road. Tall, short, thin, fat, young, old, babes, all sorts of people… The bleating of the goats taken for the sacrifice could be heard from faraway. No, no, unlike other days, looking for stuff, Seng did not run after the pilgrims. Holding the bunch of kunda flowers, even at noon, he sat on a dark stone which looked like an elephant's belly.

After cleaning the dishes and utensils used during the lunch, and after wiping clean the kitchen, Padma told her mother, 'I am going to look for flowers. The Goddess wants white flowers.'

Stupefied, Yashobai looked at her.

Pointing towards Seng, who was sitting at the Mekhela Ujowa Road, Padma said, 'I won't go alone. Look, Seng

Bawna is sitting there. He also knows where to find white flowers…"

Her mother looked upwards. Seeing Seng, a smile appeared on her lips. 'Go, go… You spend most of your time in the dark room… Oh, aai, go, go…'

***

Iss… Today, on this side of the river, there was a bunch of wild geese. The chap, chap sound of their wings and the chap, chap sound of the oars of the boats coming from the North could be heard from afar. At the end of the forest path, standing on the edge of the river filled with thorny bushes and German grass, Padmapriya noticed that Shambhudev was not there today to practise sacrifice by slicing the robab tengas.

Suddenly, the dwarf Seng noticed Shambhudev under a tamarind tree, which was covered with an old ghilalata, like a giant python coiling around the tree. He was sharpening his sword on a stone. Seng Bawna started to laugh.

Crawling though the stones, Padma reached Shambhudev. Without looking at her, he said, 'This is my own kharag. This doesn't belong to Devipeeth.' As if he was trying to convince himself.

'For sacrifice, a kharag is the ultimate weapon. A sacrifice by a sword, a bow, or a saw is average. According to scriptures, a sacrifice by a razor or a spear is the worse. When someone offers a sacrifice made by these objects, the person making the sacrifice dies.'

Seng inched near the kharag, touched the sharp edge and screamed in delight. Then he performed an elaborate mime of how the sacrifice is performed, how the kharag is used on the animal's neck.

Looking at Padma, Shambhudev smiled.

Tearing the leaves of the ghilalata plant distractingly, Padma asked Shambhudev, 'Deo, I want to offer the Goddess my own blood... I have two wishes...'

Looking at her, Shambhudev said, 'The scripture says the lower caste people can offer their own blood and invoke Chandika and Bhoirabi... But, you are a Brahmani? How would you offer the blood of your own body? You will be committing the sin of self-killing...'

Shambhudev stood up. He looked at his wrist. The hold of his fist will have to be strong. ...Ah, the other day, he had to throw three blows on a huge buffalo. The bali-data (one who offers the sacrificial animal) is now terrified... He had offered the sacrifice to save himself from his enemies.

Then, as if, he had remembered something, he looked up and stared at the girl who wanted to offer the Goddess her own blood.

The blood inside the body was boiling. Her dark hair that fell to her knees was similar to the Goddess's hair. And her legs? The naked legs beneath the muga mekhela that she wore at a height had the colour of skimmed milk.

And, the bosom of the girl who wanted to offer the blood of her bosom to the Goddess? Iss, iss, as if, two suns have ascended after having a bath in the Brahmaputra... as if, leaving behind the signs of their untamed existence on water, the suns ascended to the bank.

'Bhagawati's daughter Padma? You were looking for flowers, right? Come, I will show you where Kunda flowers bloom...'

...Screaming and hopping with joy, Seng walked ahead of them. A little ahead, they saw the people from the Garo village, who had already cleaned the buffalo sacrificed today morning before the Goddess Bhoirabi. Now, they were in the process of carrying the meat downhill. Their 'hey-ho, hey-ho' sound could be heard from afar. The crows, which were feasting on the blood and the fat and the hoof and tail strewn on the grass, also created a cacophony.

Looking at the scene, Shambhudev explained in an intense voice, 'The head of this buffalo fell towards the north. So, the bali-data is blessed. Do you know what is written in the old scriptures? ...If the head of the human sacrifice, after he is severed from his nerves, smiles, then the enemy is vanquished, all enemies disappear. If tears flow from the eyes of the severed head, even that means good luck...'

...They again heard the 'hey-ho, hey-ho' sound of the people who were carrying the meat of the sacrificed buffalo downhill.

Padmapriya screamed. 'Isn't it a sign of pain when the severed head sheds tears? Even the buffalo experiences pain.'

Shambhudev again lifted his head to look at her. This time he did not respond.

...This side of the peeth area was a dense forest. Tamarind, wild ghilalata, pama, bheleu, ah, what trees were not there? Seng stopped his dancing, came close to Padma and started to match strides with her.

'I was born in this Peeth, but I don't remember coming here even once,' she said.

'Even if you don't, your father would know this place,' Shambhudev said. 'Once your father had decorated a deodha, possessed by Bhoirabi, with a crown of wood apple leaves and garland of ghantakarna flowers... He did not eat fruits like other deodhas... He consumed the warm blood of pigeons. And then, he beat himself up with a cane rod until his skin peeled off. ...Do you know why I still remember him? When the deodha danced at the Bhoirabi temple on the edge of a sword, it sliced his feet into two.'

'Ha, ha, ha,' Seng Bawna laughed a raucous laughter... '*Bong, Bong, Bong, Bong...*'

A group of pilgrims was walking up through the jungle path. They were murmuring the Goddess's mantra...

Kamakhya barade devi neelaparvatavasini
Kamakhya barade devi neelaparvatavasini...

...All three finally stopped in front of a cave. There was so much vegetation, trees and bushes, creepers and foliage here that at times they had crouch to get ahead.

'Inside this, a little further, are the heavenly kunda flowers...'

'Here?'

'Yes, yes. Here.'

Seng screamed, 'It's dark out there. I am terrified.'

'Dark?'

'Yes, yes, dark. It was darkened by the mossy stones and the creepers. But, those kunda flowers bloom inside like clay lamps offered to the Secret Durga, Chinnamasta. ...Come, come inside, come...'

Seng Bawna started to panic. No, no, he did not want to go another step further... Leaving him there, Padmapriya entered the cave with Shambhudev, to collect a sapling of the flower that blooms with a golden hue.

...Was it a pui creeper or bandar kekowa, something coiled around Seng. He started to whimper and jump. Cautiously, Padma and Shambhudev walked into the cave filled with thorny bushes, bankuhum, thekeramahi tree, bushes of bhekuri, wild dhekia, and ghilalata... There was a wild smell everywhere. The same mysterious scent pervaded the Dham when they poured scent on 108 pots of water during the purification ritual of Ambubashi... From where was the scent emanating...? From where? Everywhere, there was the Goddess's blood.

...Was there a spring nearby? There was a *kal, kal* sound of running water. From here, the Brahmaputra looked like the crumpled garment that a newlywed bride wore on her honeymoon night.

...After touching the bandarkekowa leaves, Seng started to jump and scratch himself everywhere.

***

When Padmapriya returned from the cave with a kunda flower sapling, her hair covered her face. She ran and stood next to Seng, who was still scratching himself. Shambhudev was still inside. They heard his intense, emotional voice, 'There are saplings of golden flowers here… The golden flower that the Goddess wears during her dance. …With my kharag, I will clear the creepers. You would recognise the way, wouldn't you? Wouldn't you?'

The pollen of which flowers were on her body?

What was this scent?

The scent like the scented water to purify the menstruating Goddess…

What was this scent?

What was this scent?

Like the smell of spilt blood that wafted from the Brahmaputra, what was this stench?

Holding the sapling of the kunda flower in one hand, and dragging Seng, who was still suffering from skin rash, with the other, Padma hurriedly walked back home.

***

She noticed the faces of the boys who tied the horns and the legs of the buffalo at the sacrificial enclosure. Another group of people were pouring water on the neck of the beast to make the flesh softer. Oh, oh, oh, ropes were tied to the struggling beast's horns and legs... Helpless creature. Look, she now hurried towards Shambhudev. His kharag fell from his hand. With her long nails, she scratched Shambhudev's bare chest.

'Iss, iss, iss, don't you have any sympathy... iss, iss, iss...'

On both her hands was Shambhudev's blood...

Padmapriya woke up with a start... What was that dream? What was the dream she dreamt? At midnight, she left her room and stood next to her mother's bed. Lifting the mosquito net, she woke her mother and then holding her, started to weep. Yashobai woke up with a start. She asked desperately, 'Iss, iss, my daughter, why do you cry? Why do you cry? ... Has the mark on your back spread? If something has actually happened, I will send you for treatment, why do you cry? Aai?'

Clasping her mother's hand, she said, 'I am terrified. I am terrified.'

'Oh, why are you terrified? Why are you terrified?'

Bhagawati, who was sleeping in the next room, lifted his mosquito net and came out. Hearing him get down from the bed, Padmapriya clung to Yashobai's neck.

Bhagawati screamed. 'If the aapi is scared to stay alone in the dark room, why don't you go and give her company?'

'No, no, I am not scared. I am not scared. I can stay alone...' Then she started to weep again.

Spent, a little while later, she went back to her own bed and closed the door.

All night, Bhagawati and Yashobai sat on the floor and discussed the situation. They even mulled over the plan to write to Bhagawati's brother, Chandranath, who was studying Sanskrit in Varanasi, to come home. They could not arrive at a solution.

Chapter Two

ONE

Dhang! Dhang!! Dhang!!!

Bhe-pu! Bhe-pu!! Bhe-pu!!!

A procession descended from Devipeeth. The sound of conch, bells and cymbals spread everywhere. The households on the foothills all came out and cheered the procession.

Bhe-pu! Bhe-pu! Dhang! Dhang! Dhang!! Holding kuhh stalks and a garland of tulsi, look, it was Nandankumar Daloi, descending from the hill with his relatives. After completing the shradh for the seven generations of ancestors, Daloi was coming down to offer pinda in the river. Nanda Daloi was tall, lithe, and extremely fair.

...Those days the Brahman families who lived surrounding the Kamakhya temple on the Nilachal Hill had started marrying off their daughters to households in the plains. Now, Daloi's daughter Bhanumati was going to a rich household in the valley. ...Those who gathered outside their houses to watch the procession, discussed among each other. 'This would be a huge wedding. This would be a huge wedding... Today, people are just climbing up, like lines of ants...'

Yashobai had already gone up. The same way Padma was Lavanya's best friend, Yashobai too was on very good terms with the family of Nanda Doloi. Padma and her father were outside.

...Then, with a scream, Padma ran indoors. Bhagawati understood. She had noticed Bhubaneshwar. Yes, yes, with the procession, there he was, Bhubaneshwar. The same healthy look. The thick hair on his head was the same, and there was a thick brush of hair under his nose. Bhagawati could also see the colour of the border of the man's Shantipuri dhoti.

...Iss, with such expectations, they had chosen him to be their son-in-law. How much they argued with each other while discussing the scriptures! How many arguments they had about the gomed gem? There was such a big debate between the father-in-law and the son-in-law about whether a gomed was useful to men or whether it was useful to women to get rid of jealously, hatred, anger, and wrath.

Like the colour of cow meat, Bhagawati had given him a gomed stone set in a gold ring. Look, the ring still sparkled on his finger. ...There were complications of Rahu in the birth chart. Hurdles in work, desire for other's women? Iss, iss, iss, Bhawagati remembered everything. Look, look, he did not want to turn his face towards the house. He was trying to hide his face among other people.

'Haramzada, Haramzada (despicable man), kukur! Kukur (dog)... Your... Your clan...' iss, iss, a string of abuse words gathered around his mouth. Iss, iss, iss, iss, why did these words want to come out of the mouth at this age?

The *dhang, dhang* sound of the cymbal went downwards. Like the buzzing of the bees, the murmuring of the procession too went downwards.

Bhagawati screamed, 'Oi, Padmapriya, if you hide in the dark cell, you will turn into a skeleton in the dark cell itself. Listen, since he is here, seeing an opportunity, it would be better, if we can talk to him. Aren't two-three women of Brahmins-Gohains staying happily together in Batarhaat Dakhala? Together... happily...'

***

Bhagawati did not think that Padmapriya would actually get ready to attend the wedding. ...He could not believe his own eyes. Look, she was standing on the threshold.

...The garment of paat that she wore during her wedding day suited her so well. ...On her forehead what was that mark? The sindur that the Jatadhari Vaishnabi procured for her, to seduce men? The ultimate means to dominate the husband, the sparkling scarlet mark on the forehead, prepared with sindur and the blood of one's chest. Like the blood-shot eyes of Goddess Chamunda, the sparkling scarlet spot. Certainly. Certainly the sign of some Vaishnavi's mantra...

Despairing, Bhagawati screamed, 'Aai, you really want to go there?'

He came forward and patting her head, he added, 'I was just joking... aai, I...'

Bending her head, Padmapriya listened to her father. She did not respond. Then she walked out of the house. In the last two years, no one had seen her walk like this.

Uncertain, Bhagawati stood there like a man hit by thunder.

TWO

As soon as she was at the wedding, everyone's eyes were on her. ...In the last two years, she had not attended a single wedding on the hill. It was as if, the community saw her for the first time today. She was the first girl in Devipeeth who had been abandoned by her husband. She was the first.

...Iss, iss, what kind of looks were those. As if, forcefully removing all her clothes, they all were set to make her stand naked among them.

Just then, Lavanya came running. 'Come, come, you sit in the room where they are dicing betel nuts. You don't have to sit here.'

The room where the betel nuts and leaves were stored was in a corner, next to the road the householders used to fetch water from the Brahmaputra. There were stone stairs on the road. Outside, the cooks were preparing a feast. Someone even hung a goatskin just peeled from the goat butchered for the feast. As the evening approached, with the crowd swelling, and with the beating of the drums, people could hardly hear each other.

They both descended the stairs. It was a full moon night. Like the breast of a fair maiden who had just a bath in the Brahmaputra, the moon on the sky was completely naked.

Bhe-pu! Bhe-pu! Bhe-pu!

Beating the cymbal, a Bapu (elderly man who performs religious rituals) descended from the stairs. In his hand was a pot of holy water from some or other puja. On his head was a garland of tulsi.

Bhe-pu! Bhe-pu! Bhe-pu!

There were not many people in the room, where the betel nuts and leaves were stored.

Giving her a murha to sit, Lavanya told her, 'It's getting dark. So, not many would be here... Listen, I will invite him here. He will surely talk. ...Whatever you want to tell him, tell him clearly. About expenses... or, or... Even though they are our relatives, we cannot tolerate this injustice.'

Bhe-pu! Bhe-pu! Bhe-pu!

A smart girl, Lavanya then whispered into her ear, 'Not only through speech, try to converse with your body also. When someone talks to a young lover like this, all his orthodoxy, pride, anger and wrath comes to naught. The tiger turns into a mouse.'

Padmapriya did not answer. Lavanya climbed up to fetch Bhubaneshwar.

In Devipeeth it was as if there were a divine manifestation in the moonlit night... spreading silver dust on the water, making a *kal, kal* sound, as if the Goddess herself were dancing.

...On her breasts was a methani of kunda flowers.

...Iss, kunda flowers, kunda flowers! Look, everywhere, there were kunda flowers. On the Goddess's breasts, the methani of kunda flowers.

Dhang! Dhang! Dhang!

Bhe-pu! Bhe-pu!

Carrying water for his puja, the deo climbed up.

***

First published as '*Debipeethar Tej*'. The text, translated by the author herself, as 'Under the Shadow of Kamakhya', appeared in an anthology *Under the Shadow of Kamakhya*, in 2005.

Delhi, 5 November 1991

Ismail Sheikh was in his old shoe store. He wore a loose shirt, and corduroy trousers, which had several patches on them. His wry face looked like the face of an old horse. He had purchased the trousers from a second-hand clothes store near Jama Masjid.

As he was about to gather his belongings, Ganga Dhasla, who carried a gas light ahead of wedding processions, stood before him dragging his broken chappal. Unlike the other days, Ismail did not make the comment, 'Throw them away. If you cannot, I will do it for you. *Nalayak kahika*... (worthless person).'

However, like other days, Ismail noticed the huge scar on Ganga Dhasla's leg. A grimy bandage covered the scar. This happened after the incident during the wedding at a Seth's house on Bungalow Road. Nobody in Prem Gali has forgotten what happened after a band of youngsters got drunk and in their enthusiastic dance, fell upon the group of people carrying the gas lights. One died on the spot. Ganga Dhasla barely got out alive. Ismail bit his tongue every time he saw the leg.

Meanwhile, two of Ismail Sheikh's customer-friends appeared at the door: the mechanic from Andha Mughal, Pappu Gupta, and Angrez Seth from Prem Gali.

Angrez Seth had a huge moustache; his colour was like a ripe fruit. He was around 80. He was a mysterious inhabitant of Delhi's Prem Gali. It was said that like the Bhil dacoits, he escaped from prison by breaking the walls with his bare hands. He used to hang out with some notorious criminals from Farrukhabad. Once, it was said, he was even arrested in a murder case.

As the colour of his skin was like that of a foreigner, there were rumours about his birth. People said when Sir Thomas Metcalfe was the Resident of Delhi, Angrez Seth's grandfather used to look after Metcalfe Sahab's favourite Napoleon House. People even claimed that in the conspiracy to poison Metcalfe, who wanted to destroy the entire clan of Badshah Bahadur Shah, even Angrez Seth's elder brother was also involved. Was Metcalfe really poisoned? This no one knew. Around this time, people said, Angrez Seth's grandmother had an affair with a white soldier.

***

Pappu Gupta, Ganga Dhasla, Angrez Seth, all gathered at Ismail Sheikh's shop every day to gossip. Today, however, the conversations did not flow. Another member of the party, Himmat Singh, had just joined the Army. Ganga Dhasla and

Pappu too had been trying for the same job, but to no avail. Both were green with envy.

Today, they did not have much work. Still, they both arrived and sat next to Ismail. There was a quarter bottle in Ganga's pocket. He went up to Ismail and whispered something in his ears. They then got up and left the shop. They stood facing the wall of the nearby building, which was littered with posters from the recent elections. Ganga fished the bottle out of his pocket. Each of them took a few large gulps. Then Ismail Sheikh returned and resumed his work. Angrez Seth was looking at the goings-on with his large copper eyes. Suddenly, he stood up and like a beaten dog chased after Ganga, and snatched the bottle from his pocket. Ganga had a small frame. With his loose pajama and dirty bush shirt, he looked just like a skeleton. He could barely stop himself from falling face down. Tucking the bottle in his own pocket, Angrez Seth offered him an indulgent smile. His two golden teeth sparkled among the decaying yellowed ones.

Like other days, today too, no one objected to Angrez Seth. He said, '*Aare yaar, yahan toh mil baat ke khane ki reet hain* (my friend, here the rule is to share and enjoy).'

Ismail, Ganga Dhasla, Pappu remained silent. By now, the streetlights were on. The number of vehicles coming from GT Road started to wane. All remained quiet. Ismail was repairing a pair of shoes for Angrez Seth. The streetlight, which was just above his head, was bright. To work on the minute details, he had a special eyeglass. He removed the pair from his pocket and wore it. The streetlight was just above his shop; like an umbrella standing above his head, it illuminated the shop. He also fixed a nail on Ganga's chappal.

Prem Gali was a bizarre place. It opened up to one of Delhi's busiest roads, GT Road. Most inhabitants here were old residents of Delhi. The municipality had marked a few houses. The interiors of some of the old buildings were so dark, it were as if time itself, in a blaze, had turned them into pitch black. The lane was filled with motor mechanics, tailors, vegetable vendors, workers of a bidi-making factory, and labourers who worked in the ironwork factories in Andha Mughal. Some of the workers lived in old, rented miyanis (attics). They were, however, not of the Sahashi tribe. Those people from the Sahashi tribe in Andha Mughal were so criminal-minded that there was a time when they had to visit the police station every day to mark their attendance. All residents of Andha Mughal had to go to the police station to mark their attendance.

The place was filled with rickshaw-pullers, construction labourers, vendors who sold vegetables on wheeled carts, launderers, tailors and sellers of rubber chappals. As dusk fell, people who worked in various parts of the city were returning to Prem Gali. Some pulled khatiyas (string cots) from their homes to places under the streetlights. Soon, they will gather to play cards there. Others, meanwhile, started setting up their coal stoves and flour-mixing pans right on the street.

Suddenly, Ganga Dhasla and Pappu screamed. 'Look, that's Bibi Vimala Chaudhury! Bibi Vimala Chaudhury.'

Vimala.

Those surrounding Ismail now gawked at the lamppost in front of them.

Yes, yes. It was Vimala Chaudhury, in a khadi sari, carrying a khadi bag. Her short hair was above her shoulders. Lipstick on her lips. Kajal around her eyes. Kolhapuri chappals on her feet. Making a *chatap*, *chatap* sound, Vimala was coming towards the lamppost where the group gathered. Behind her was her autistic brother, who walked with a limp. Saliva ran from both ends of his mouth. He could not match strides with Vimala. Passing by Ismail's shop, Vimala walked towards Roshanara Road.

Ismail, Angrez Seth, Ganga Dhasla, Pappu, everybody gaped at her and her autistic brother with open mouths. Nobody made a sound. Only when she disappeared in the circle ahead did Angrez Seth open his mouth: 'She did not get married. The marriage was fixed. But when the bridegroom asked for dowry, she gave him a good slap.'

Ismail said, 'Her mother lives with her. I have heard that her brothers help with cash. They both got married and fled. There is nobody to look after the speech-impaired brother.'

Ismail Sheikh added, 'She is metric pass. Works in the party paper *Awaaz*. Works very hard.'

All of them corroborated, 'Yes, yes. She works in *Awaaz*. She is metric pass.'

'Age?'

Pappu screamed. 'More than 30. When I was working at the kerosene depot in "Pili Building" (yellow building), she would come to fetch kerosene, wearing a sari.'

Angrez Seth said, 'Now, how will she get married? Giving her the responsibility of her mother and the gunga brother, others have washed their hands.'

All of them screamed together, 'Yes, yes, all have washed their hands.'

Angrez Seth's face lit up with a bewildering smile. He said, '*Bahadur ladki* (brave girl).'

The others screamed together, '*Bahadur ladki*! Why?'

'She has earned praise by helping Himmat Singh get into the Army. Ganga and Pappu, pushing both of you, Himmat went to the *fauj*. You will die with your broken chappals.'

Ganga and Pappu hung their heads. Their financial condition was not good.

The chappal fixed, Ismail Sheikh returned it to Ganga. He said, 'Didn't Himmat's father, Daya mochi (cobbler), ask him to gather some shoes and sit in a corner. There was no hope of him getting into the Army.'

Ganga said, 'We have seen the father and son fight and break each other's heads.'

Angrez Seth said, 'Now Daya Singh cannot fight anymore. Cancer.'

'Cancer.'

All of them kept quiet for a while.

Angrez Seth, however, did not stop taunting Ganga and Pappu, 'Listen, Ganga and Pappu, didn't you go to Lal Quila (Red Fort) to get into the *fauj*?'

Ganga said, 'We did, we did.'

'Listen, this time, you go and fall on Bibi Vimala's feet. Otherwise, you will end your lives eating leftovers, like the dogs in the Roshanara Garden.'

After entering the *fauj*, with the BKF, Himmat Singh too was in Jaffna for a while. After that, he was back in Delhi on a short leave.

… For the people of Prem Gali, for a few days, this was the only subject of gossip.

'…The local girl performed a magic trick. Himmat Singh got lucky. If he had not met her, he would have spent his whole life amidst torn shoes. Now, he wears brand-new footwear.'

'…Wah! Himmat Singh's look has changed completely. Now, he has put on weight. Even his short hair is dense and better looking. Under his nose, there is a thick, slick moustache…' Nobody could recognise it was the same man who roamed the streets of Andha Mughal, Majnu Ka Tilla, Katar Neel, Butler Street.

Returning home for the first time, Himmat Singh showered his respect on Vimala Chaudhury. From carrying the grocery from the ration shop to carrying her papers to the *Awaaz* office, he helped her in such ways that for a few days she forgot the treachery of how her brothers left, giving her the responsibility of her mother and her autistic brother. She thought secretly, if she had a son of her own, he would perhaps have helped her like this. Like all her friends who got married young, if she had married young, she too would have a young son like this. She was now 35 years old. Whenever she saw Himmat Singh, a blessing broke forth, breaking her heart.

***

When Himmat Singh returned on leave for the second time, his father Daya mochi had already shifted his shop to Butler Street. Meanwhile, the No. 6 shop on Prem Gali was filled with shiny bottles with pictures of grapes on them.

During his vacation, Himmat Singh spent most of his time with Ismail Sheikh, Angrez Seth, Ganga and Pappu. During the evening, they would sit on the stairs of the Roshanara Mazar at Roshanara Garden and chat. He had cash in his pocket, happiness in his heart. Though all of them sat and shared drinks, in their hearts, they were green with envy.

On the evening before his return to duty too, they sat on the stairs of Roshanara Mazar. All sorts of people came to this garden. Even terrorists had their secret meetings here. …In between, a constable came and sold them two quarter bottles at a discounted price.

As soon as the constable left, Angrez screamed, '*Sala, uthakar laya hoga. Inka toh kaam yahi hain. Kisi se bidi leta, kisi se paan. Yahan tak ki randiyon se bhi dalali nahin chodte!* (Bastards, they must have picked it up from somewhere. This is what they do, take a bidi from someone, take a paan from someone else. They do not even mind charging from the prostitutes as well).'

Suddenly, Ismail Sheikh said in jest, 'Aare Himmat Singh. Do ask your madam to let Ganga and Pappu enter the force. Now, everyone knows how friendly she is with the leaders.'

Hearing Ismail Sheikh, Himmat Singh was surprised. He did not utter a word. They sipped their drinks in silence.

It was as if the liquid inside the bottle decorated with colourful grape vines had clearly unveiled the fact that Ganga Dhasla, Ismail Sheikh, Pappu, Angrez, everyone was jealous about how Himmat Singh got so lucky... They were all desperate for jobs and then the boy among them, who wore a pair of torn chappals and a patchwork coat from the second-hand shop on the banks of Jamuna got lucky. It was unbelievable. Look, he was wearing shiny shoes. His hair was nicely cut. Nobody had noticed before that even his skin was so clear. He looked exactly like the boys who studied in St. Stephen's.

In their hearts, seeds of jealously turned into wild fires. They started to needle Himmat Singh. Angrez Seth was at the forefront of this. All of them were already inebriated.

Angrez said, '*Mila na ek aurat raat gujarne ke liye. Umar mein tumse badi hui toh kya hua, kaam toh tumhari aa hi jayagi* (At least you've got a woman to spend the night with. So what if she is older than you, she can still be used).'

Himmat Singh did not utter a word in his defence. For a while, he was huffing like a wounded person. Then suddenly he got up and started to throttle Angrez Seth. Though Angrez was getting older, he had not completely lost his legendary strength. Everyone knew him to be the hero of those horrible tales from the past. He landed a punch on Himmat Singh and threw him at a distance. Pappu and Ganga stood between them to stop the fight from escalating.

Then they started hurling abuses at each other in the choicest of words. In the magic of those words, Vimala, who had earned respect from people by slapping the boy who dared to ask for dowry, and by saying that she would never get married, was now naked, in the bed of the party leader. On the other hand, Angrez Seth, before whom nobody dared to mention his criminal past, was outed as a murderer 10 times.

***

In November 1991 too, Himmat Singh had returned home on leave. This time he had returned to Delhi from Akhnoor in Kashmir. He brought a woollen shawl for Vimala. Wearing the shawl, she strolled around the open terrace next to the barsati. Her eyes turned moist. All these years she did so much for her own family, but nobody showed her so much love by buying her a woollen shawl. Instead, her two elder brothers had washed their hands of the matter, after putting the responsibility of the autistic brother on her head. They thought their duties were over once they dumped some cash in her fist for the wellbeing of her mother and brother.

Her eyes turned moist when she wrapped the shawl around her body.

This time, while collecting news for *Awaaz*, Himmat Singh even accompanied her to several places, including Jama Masjid and Sarai Kale Khan.

She was determined to find the truth behind the story where, in a fight between two political parties, the slum hutments near Ganda Nullah were gutted in a blaze. For a whole week, Himmat Singh walked with her like a shadow.

In everything, going to the hospital to check on the burn victims, listening to their versions of the story, arguing with the police, writing the description of the slum which had turned into a crematorium, checking on the facts, Himmat Singh was with her like a shadow.

...Vimala could not even believe her own eyes. She had helped make a life. Truly, she had been able to pick up Himmat Singh from the gutter.

***

This had happened in June last year. By then, she had visited many places looking for a job for Himmat Singh. From Sheikh Sarai to Sarai Rohilla, to Kabbadi Bazaar to as far as Nizamuddin, she did not leave a single party office.

With this experience, she even had planned to write a long story for the paper. No, no, there was no hope for young people in this country, no hope at all. The story, however, remained unwritten. One day in the office, she met Kashinath, an old leader from the same constituency.

Seeing Vimala, Kashinath shouted, 'Vimala, I remember you. You had come to me several times looking for a job for Himmat Singh.'

'Yes, yes, I remember. Your office is in Sheikh Sarai! From Prem Gali, Sheikh Sarai must be around 20 kilometres. Please consider. You are the leader. Can you not offer unemployment benefits to metric pass unemployed youths? Himmat Singh's father is a cobbler. He has cancer. Now recovering a bit, he is back on his job. The old man has worked very hard to make his son pass the 10th.'

Kashinath repeated, 'Himmat Singh has passed the metric. Wah, wah, Himmat Singh has passed the metric.'

Vimala did not like how the leader Kashninath uttered the words. To tell the truth, for this leader too, she did not have any respect. She worked for the party magazine just to earn a living. In her heart, she always had the same dream. She will fly away like a bird, at the slightest of chances. Besides, the editor published her writings with such chopping and slicing that she had no option but to grit her teeth.

She locked her eyes on Kashinath's and said, 'Can you not really arrange for an unemployment benefit?'

Kashinath answered as if he was blaming everyone else. 'In this country, where lakhs of people are under-employed, it's foolish to even think about unemployment benefits.'

She gazed into Kashinath's eyes. The man was very thin and very lanky. His age was around 50. His cheekbones were high, but his cheeks had caved in. the eyes were deep-set, but bright. It was as if looking at someone, he could read the person's whole history. Some people did not need an explanation; they understood it with their own intelligence and cunning. Kashinath was such an ambitious man. If someone were ambitious, he had to be unsatisfied. During the municipal corporation election, he moved heaven and earth to get a ticket, but the party did not give him one.

His supporters were really surprised when Kashinath did not get the ticket. The seat went to Sarai Rohilla's Ramlal. He was a known criminal from Sarai Rohilla. He was the owner of a restaurant known for cabaret dance. There were several cases against him in the court. People said there was also a murder case among them. The neighbourhood was terrified of his very name, just like a villain in a Hindi movie. His eyes were bright. He wore a pair of dark glasses all the time, even during the winter. He drove around in a huge foreign car. He got the ticket for the corporate elections and with the help of his thugs, even won the seat.

Unhappy, Kashinath stopped going to the party office for some time. Well-wishers even suggested that he should change parties. He, however, knew the sad stories of some politicians after they started hopping parties. So, after roaming around the lanes of Andha Mughal, Roshanara Road and Singh Sabha Road, he returned to the party office.

Vimala led Kashinath to the wall of the cement godown next to the party office. She begged, 'I am desperate to get Himmat Singh a job. I will explain it to you. Please come to my house in Prem Gali once. I live with my old mother. There is also a dumb brother at home. Please come to my house once. I will explain everything to you.'

***

Kashinath came to visit Vimala in the evening. He sat on the lone iron chain in the house. He sat comfortably, putting one of his legs on the top of the other. He looked clean and fresh. He did not wear the regular khadi kurta and pajama. He wore an old ash-coloured pathan suit. He had just a few strands of hair on his head. But his mustache was thick and dark. Even the colour of his skin was very clear.

As part of her work, earlier, a few leader-types had visited her house, but no one at the level of Kashinath. Vimala did not want to leave any stones unturned in taking care of the guest.

Even her ailing mother left her bed, and huffing and puffing, bowed her head in front of Kashinath.

Vimala led Kashinath to the dirty footpath between the coal godown and a ration shop. She said, 'Listen, just here, Daya Singh, Himmat Singh's father, had his shoe repair shop on an old gunnysack. After he fell ill, he shifted the shop to Andha Mughal.'

'Ill?'

'Yes, yes, he has cancer of the intestines.'

Vimala and Kashinath walked ahead and stood at the dirty spot where Daya Singh mochi had his makeshift shop.

Kashinath asked, 'His treatment?'

'An administrative officer of the Hindu Rao Hospital was Daya Singh's regular customer. For the last 10 years, Daya Singh had been cleaning his shoes. He got the chance to get admission in the hospital with the help of this officer. I was told the officer himself went to the OPD to get Daya Singh his card. He also informed the doctor in charge. After that I myself have witnessed the struggle for his life. The condition of the family is indescribable. After staying in hospital for one long year, after a part of his intestines was operated on, he could come back to life. For the last one year, he is going through chemotherapy. All his hair is gone. When he returned to his spot here after the hospital, I could barely recognise him. Then he shifted his shop to Andha Mughal. Now he is extremely weak, cannot even walk properly, and, and...'

Kashinath asked, 'And what?'

'... After completing his 10th, Himmat Singh has become a burden on his father... Please find him a job in the *fauj*. The mochi will be very proud. The sick man is alive just for this one hope. Himmat Singh has two other brothers studying in school. The condition is unspeakable.'

Vimala walked ahead to the exact spot where once Himmat Singh's father had his shop.

Meanwhile, the labourers who worked on the mills, the contractors, vendors, cobblers, jamadars (sweepers), kabadiwalas (waste pickers) and barbers had returned to their respective rooms. Some were gossiping, sitting on cots outside. Some had brought out their playing cards. A bunch of half-naked kids were playing cricket even amidst the rush.

Then the children went home. A mixed scent of coal, kerosene and freshly baked rotis wafted everywhere. Outside the Ghulam Store, next to the coal godown, the '*angrezi videshi dawaiyon ke vikreta* (English and foreign medicine seller)', which the people of Prem Gali knew as No. 6 Shop, there was a group of grotesque men in a line. What kind of bottles were those, with a picture of grapes within a red border on the label? Those listless men made a beeline in front of No. 6 Shop. Vimala and Kashinath noticed their legs like logs gutted in a fire, their dirty kurta-kameez and their hair filled with grime and dust.

Kashinath averted his eyes and said, 'So Vimala, Daya Singh used to sit right here?'

'Yes. We know him from childhood. Though he repaired shoes, he is an educated man. He himself helped Himmat Singh in his studies.'

Kashinath inched closer to her and said in a consolatory tone, 'I will put him in the *fauj*. Col. Maan Singh stays beyond the Yamuna river. I know him.'

Giving Vimala his assurance, Kashinath left the house. Coming out to see him off, Vimala noticed how the line of the men to buy those long bottles had become longer, as if it was a broken ladder. The labourers who pushed the hand-carts in the vegetable market had returned bent over like monkeys. Perhaps they were hauling cement bags today.

In the brightness of the streetlight, the cement specks on their hair sparkled brightly, as if they were wearing some kind of caps. The labourers who worked in the trampoline factory in Sarai Kale Khan had also stood in the line in front of the shop. They may have had some work this side. Even the labourers who carried the gas lights in the Mohan Band Party stood in the line in front of the No. 6 Shop of '*angrezi videshi dawaiyon ke vikreta*'.

***

Two constables were loitering in front of the shop. As the line, like a broken ladder, started to grow like the tail of Hanuman in Lanka, both the constables disappeared from the spot. Pointing towards the policemen, who left without uttering a word, a thin labourer said, '*Inn salon ne iss chay number dukan se bohat munafa khaya hain* (These bastards have earned a lot of profits from this No. 6 shop)'.

Another added, '*Aare bhai, inn pyado ka kya baat karta hain, yahan se upar ke neta tak hissa jata hain* (Brother, forget these foot soldiers; from here, a share also goes to the people at the top).'

Vimala and Kashinath heard this. Now, taking leave from Vimala, Kashinath started to walk fast towards Roshanara Road. As he walked with his back straight, the pathan suit he wore appeared loose on him.

***

This happened around three months back. To get Himmat Singh a job in the *fauj*, Vimala went to Seelampur in an auto, with Kashinath.

During the entire journey, Vimala remembered the straight hair that had started to grow on Daya Singh's head. Before the cancer, he had long hair, salt and pepper long hair. It was all gone after the disease. Now, the new-grown hair had the colour of human bone after cremation. The auto sped towards the Jamuna Bridge. In her reverie, Vimala had forgotten about Kashinath, who sat close to her, touching elbows.

Then Vimala realised that grabbing her hand, Kashinath was trying to take it towards his thigh. Her hand came in contact with a piece of flesh, hard as iron. She was shocked. This piece of flesh, which was hard like an iron latch, was Kashinath's genitalia. She would often forget the fact that she was a woman. She felt as if someone had beaten her with a stick and reminded her that she was a woman. Vimala thought it was as if the two snakes that lay coiled on her two breasts woke up baring their fangs. But just for a moment. Filled with shame and hatred, she started to recoil. For the reminder of the road, she was tortured by the genitalia as hard as an iron latch and the newly grown hair on Daya mochi's head after the chemo.

***

There was almost a war of words between Vimala and Kashinath on their return after meeting Colonel Sahib in

Seelampur. She wanted to return by bus. Kashinath wanted to take an auto. Finally, when the Colonel Sahib took Vimala's side, Kashinath agreed to take a bus. The bus stop was just in front of the Colonel's house. From here, a lot of buses went to the bus station and from the bus station, there were a number of buses to GT Road.

***

With the help of Seelampur's Colonel Sahib, Himmat Singh got into the *fauj* easily. With this, Kashinath found an easy and available excuse to visit Vimala's house. Making excuses like visiting her old mother or her autistic brother, he started to drop by Vimala's house often.

One day, he carried a bottle wrapped in a paper under his arm. He told Vimala, 'There are children in my house. As soon as I bring out the bottle, my wife starts hurling abuses. She starts to make noises, starts breaking the pots, starts pulling her hair, unnecessary drama.'

Saying this, Kashinath gave her a signal with his eyes. Vimala understood the signal. She realised it wouldn't be wise to make this man unhappy. With just a request, he got Himmat Singh a job in the *fauj*. There was no one in Andha Mughal and Prem Gali who could do something like this. ...So many of them burn their skin, tear their shoes, bloody their very soul, just looking for a job. No, no, she had to indulge the man's request. Then she remembered her ailing mother and she was uncertain.

Coughing her dry coughs, would she be able to wait on him all through the night? And, her dumb brother? Would she be able to send him to her elder brother's place for a few days? Perched in her house, Kashinath started to drink until late in the night.

***

Looking at the activities of the drunk man, sitting next to him, Vimala kept a vigil.

It was January 1990 when Kashinath first carried the bottle wrapped in a paper under his arm. This went on until November 1991.

Nodding off to sleep, while sitting on her bed, Vimala's ailing mother would sometimes scream, 'Did the man leave?'

Shrinking, Vimala would answer, '*Chup, chup* (quiet).'

In the light, sometimes Vimala would see his face, which was puffed up. And his eyes would want to dig deep and enter inside Vimala's body, as if, her body was a river and the man was swimming there. Sometimes, he would leave the remainder of the bottle with her, so that he could return the next day to finish the content... Like a piece of stale meat, she sat there, static and cold. As if, some invisible rope tied her hands and legs.

Was there a way?

Was there a way?

Should she move to Sheikh Sarai or Sarai Rohilla? Her elder brother lived in Sheikh Sarai. They too were impoverished. He worked in a soap factory. And the sister-in-law, scared that they would have to take care of her sick mother and autistic brother, would not even look towards their house. The other brother lived somewhere near Sarai Kale Khan. He was a clerk in Rail Bhawan. Even he was impoverished.

...Actually, Vimala's family came from somewhere in Farrukhabad. Her father worked in Birla Mill. He was very particular about education. Every morning, everyone in the house recited the dohas from *Ramcharitmanas*. When they were young, the owner of the mill had given this tenement in Prem Gali to her father.

Desperate, sitting next to Kashinath, who was holding a glass of the liquor, Vimala had finally decided. Even if for a few days, all three of them would go to her brother's place in Sarai Kale Khan. She was sure he would understand her plight.

One day, her mother said, 'It is everyone's duty to help the family of the man suffering from cancer. To top it, he is a leader.'

Vimala uttered the words, 'Yes, yes, he is a leader.'

One day, her mother, coughing her constant cough, dragging herself from the bed, stood outside the door. But the cough did not stop. For a long time, she stood there, coughing her cough in a rhythm. Finally, Vimala got up and helped her back to the bed.

Oh, it was torture to sit there drooping and yawning. It was a torture to sit next to a drunk man. She was already free of that fearful biological feeling. The two snakes that sat coiled on her two breasts had already disappeared. …Now, in her mind resonated just bitterness and dissatisfaction.

In the beginning, Kashinath would come at eight in the evening and would leave by 10. Slowly, he started to delay by one hour. One evening, inebriated, he screamed, '*Sala, ullu ka pattha, haramzaada* (fool, son of a fool, bastard), could he run? Last year, four hundred boys ran after the ambulance. …Could he run? *Sala*.'

Vimala said, 'Why do you curse him?'

'Just like that. Sala, was his chest size 91 centimetres? At the most, it was 80 centimetres… The Major from Rajasthan who came for the recruitment… *Sala, suar ka baccha*… (fool, son of a pig)'

'Tch, tch, why do you curse?'

'Why not? Why not? He said…'

'What did he say?'

No, no, Vimala did not want to hear anything about it… Never…

***

The glitter of the No. 6 Shop just increased. The shop was filled with quarter bottles. There were some orange bottles as well. As if, someone poured silver bubbles on the colour orange. For the labourers, khalasis of Sarai Rohilla, Majnu Ka Tila, Butler Street, Old Sabji Mandi, Singh Sabha Road and Roshanara Road, it was not just an ayurvedic tonic; it was a life-giving drink. Sometime, the line of customers would reach as far as Ismail Sheikh's shop. Sometime, some customers would even purchase cheap shoes from Ismail Sheikh. It worked well for Ismail. Often the half-naked labourers would take a shortcut through Roshanara Road via Andha Mughal to catch their buses. Under their arms, they would carry the cheap canvas shoes and in their hands, the bottle bearing the picture of grape vines.

***

As Diwali approached, the No. 6 Shop witnessed more activity than ever before. The bottles with the pictures of grape vines on them started to disappear one by one. Uncountable bottles arrived and uncountable bottles vanished.

***

On 5 November, Himmat Singh arrived from Akhnoor to celebrate Diwali. In the morning, everyone saw him escort his father to the Hindu Rao Hospital. In the evening, there was a gathering at Ismail Sheikh's shop. The colour of strong-armed Ismail Sheikh's body was clear. He had long hair and a beard like a Sikh youth. And he did wear a turban. The hair reached up to his shoulders. He wore a pair of denim jeans purchased from Jamuna Bazaar and from the second-hand shops outside Jama Masjid. Though age was catching up on him, he liked to stay young in his jeans.

Though Ganga was thin and lanky, he too loved to dress up like the heroes of the Hindi movies. He too purchased second-hand clothes from Jamuna Bazaar. He too wore denim jeans. Sometimes he wore colourful bush shirts. Pappu did not care about sartorial aesthetics. He too wore clothes from the secondhand shops in Jamuna Bazaar or the shops outside Jama Masjid. But his pajama was always dirty. On his shirt, there were food stains.

This Diwali, since Himmat Singh's return, they were seen together at the stairs of the Roshanara Mazar at Roshanara Garden during the night. Their jokes, laughter, their screaming and shouting could be heard from afar.

***

5 November 1991. Early morning, some people from the party paper started knocking on Vimala's door. When the mother-daughter duo opened the door, they saw Habib photographer and several others outside. Habib worked in *Awaaz*. He came forward and said, 'So far, we have heard that more than 100 have died just in Hindu Rao Hospital alone.'

Vimala screamed, 'Died?'

The other two men with Habib screeched, 'Liquor, *jehrila daru* (poisonous alcohol).'

Vimala got ready in a minute. Her mother said, 'Don't worry, go.'

Even her brother stood near the doorway. Saliva dripped from the corners of his mouth.

Wearing a khadi sari and carrying a large khadi bag, she stood on the GT Road bus stand with Habib and the other reporters. Vimala was convinced that this was just another accident that kept happening in Delhi. They got down near Hansraj College and took the road in front of the Sabji Mandi post office towards Hindu Rao Hospital.

Her heart started to flutter once they reached the hospital. It was full of people running around, screaming and shouting, whining and crying. There was not an inch of space around the Emergency.

A mob was arguing with the police about whether the bodies of the two men who died on the way to the hospital should be shifted to the morgue or should be taken to the crematorium directly.

Vimala ran towards a doctor busy in the Emergency and accosted him, 'How many died so far? Sir, how many died so far?'

'We have admitted 119 people. A lot of them died; 105 of them are fighting for their lives. Look, they keep coming, keep coming. Don't disturb…don't disturb.'

A large mob pushed her towards the corner of the emergency. One of the victims started to vomit uncontrollably outside the hospital and passed away on the spot. Pushing through the noises, the screams, and the jostle of the half-naked relatives of the victims, who looked like beggars on the street, Vimala inched towards the eye wards on the first floor. The eye ward of the Hindu Rao Hospital had been converted into an emergency ward for the victims of poisoned hooch. Somehow stepping out of the melee, she stood outside the ward that looked like a cave.

There, Vimala came face to face with the terrible sight. All the patients who lay on the beds in the ward had gone blind. A police officer was on guard outside.

The nurses, who were busy at work, did not allow her to enter the ward. On everyone's face, there was suppressed excitement and fear. It was, as if, the poison affected half of the population of Delhi. She was finally allowed to enter the ward after she brandished her identity card and requested profusely. She walked towards the beds.

However, Habib photographer was not allowed to follow Vimala. There were police photographers.

Look, there, one patient was about to die just in front of her. The doctor, who was giving him mouth-to-mouth CPR to revive him, stood there helplessly.

...The man died in front of her. The screaming and howling of the man's family members made Vimala numb again. What was this? What was happening?

...No, no, she had to walk ahead and collect the news. Even during the riots in 1984, she had gone to Jehangir Puri and Kalyan Puri to see the blood-soaked turbans of the people who died in the massacre. She herself took the pictures of ransacked houses, the skeleton of a torched motorbike...

But this? This was an impossible sight... More than impossible.

***

'What's the name? What was his name?' Vimala asked the young man who stood next to the patient whose eyes were bandaged with cotton.

'What's his name?'

'Satish Kumar?'

'Address?'

'Sarai Rohilla'

'House Number?'

'866.'

'Relation?'

'Father.'

'How many siblings do you have?'

'Five.'

'He used to drink every day?'

'Yes. In one sitting, he finished one quarter bottle.'

'From where did he buy the liquor?'

The boy did not answer.

"What did he do for a living?'

'He used to carry the gas light with a band party.'

Then Vimala asked a woman with a baby clutched to her arm, who was standing next to another blind patient.

'Name?'

The woman was so surprised at the question that instead of answering, she squeezed the baby hard.

'Name? Name?'

'Panchdeo, Panchdeo!'

'What work did he do?'

'Rickshawwalla.'

'Address?'

'Sabji Mandi.'

'When did this happen?'

'After two hours.' Saying this, she started to whimper. 'This one quarter bottle took my husband's life.'

Immediately, the two men, who were standing guard next to another blind patient, screeched, 'The police are helping those who sold the poison. Because they too get their shares from them. ...*Sab likho paper mein, sab likho* (write everything in the newspaper, write everything), so that people's eyes are open, so that they know what others are doing.'

Now, the police who were everywhere in the ward, started to make noises. There was chaos everywhere. The nurses pushed Vimala out of the ward.

An old nurse admonished, 'These paper people have no other intention than to increase the sale of their paper. They will follow wherever there are dead bodies. *Himmat hain toh jao asli gunehgaron ko pakdo* (if you have the courage, go and catch the real culprit)...'

Crossing the wards that looked like tunnels, she came out of the hospital. The entire premises was filled with people. They pushed and shoved each other to collect the death certificates from the police PCR van. There was confusion at the verification. Yes, yes, unbelievable confusion. The police distributed death certificates the way food is distributed among the famine-affected.

Vimala stood away from the police van. Habib photographer and the other two men had already disappeared. As she tried to find a way to the police van, she noticed members of two parties shouting against the government, like vultures above dead bodies. From a group of people who were mourning the death of a family member, someone shouted, 'There is no point shouting slogans here. *Agar tum mein kuch dumkham hain toh bulao woh harami ke pillon ko jo dukan ka asli malik hain* (if you have some courage, call out that bastard who is the real owner of the shop). Don't shed crocodile tears here.'

The words hit Vimala's eardrums. ...*Abhi chillane se kuch faida nahin...Bulao woh harami ke pillon ko...* (there's no point crying now. Call those bastards here). She paced towards the morgue. Brandishing her identity car and crossing the impenetrable police cordon, her head began to spin. A woman, who was there to identify a body, fell on Vimala and started to screem, 'He would drink every day. Who knew, who knew, he would drop dead on the night of Diwali.' Even two nurses could not control her. She was alone. She started to pull Vimala's clothes, and the clothes of the nurses, and then she lost her consciousness and fell on the ground.

...Look, those were the dead bodies, which were placed on top of each other, like gunnysacks. On the chests of a few of them, there were slabs of ice like slabs of concrete. A rotten smell of blood and pus emanated from the clothes of a few of them. Vimala covered her face with the end of her sari.

……The situation turned to the worse. The relatives of the dead people jostled with each other to collect the requisition form after identifying the bodies. …Flies hovered over the bodies. If only they would take the bodies and perform the last rites. The living, meanwhile, were filled with sadness, anger and rage. What would they do? What would this mob do?

The number of people and the police started to swell. Leaving the doorway of the morgue, Vimala stood outside and tried to inhale some fresh air. Holding her stomach with her hands, she started to retch. Then she pulled a notebook from her bag and wrote down the descriptions of the events unfolding before her. In the jostle of the crowd, she could barely hold her pen. …Two policemen carried a dead body, passed by her and dumped it in the morgue, as if it was not a human being, but an animal for the slaughterhouse.

Again, she held her stomach with her hands and retched. From the interiors of her heart emerged a word, which had no definition.

Look, they have come again. The police were carrying more dead bodies for the morgue. Holding onto her khadi bag, pushing through the crowd, she walked along. Someone pulled the end of her sari, 'Madam, *aap likhe-padhe ho, madat karo* (you are an educated person, please help me). My brother died at seven last night. Since last night, we haven't received the body…'

Whom will Vimala help? Whom will she help?

The woman pointed her towards the policemen who were sitting behind a table out in the open. She said again, 'You are an educated woman. Please help. My brother started to vomit last night at 10. I brought him to Hindu Rao. His number came after one hour. By then, he was dead. Now, it's eight in the morning and the police are not returning the body.'

Vimala screamed, 'Flies are hovering over the bodies. Why wouldn't they return them?'

'They say they have not received any papers from the hospital. Ten hours have passed. I have not eaten anything. Even my two legs have given up.'

Somebody came and put up a list of dead bodies on the wall of the PCR room. The people, who were standing in groups outside, surrounded the list, like flies on a ripe mango.

The woman, who had tugged on Vimala's sari, screamed again, '*Hamara laash* (our dead body).'

The two young boys, who were roaming about purposefully among the crowd, stood next to the woman and whispered in her ear, 'What do you think? We can get you the dead body immediately.'

'*Laash dilwa sakte ho* (can you help us take possession of our dead body)?'

'*Saheb logon ke liye chai-paani ka bandobast karao* (make arrangements for some bribe for the officers). You know it is required for every kind of work, when you apply for ration card, when you want to release someone on bail... Is there any place where work can be done without cash?'

Vimala screamed, 'Tell me what you want to say.'

The two teenage ruffians disappeared in the crowd. Vimala followed them. She heard the loudspeaker announcement from the Delhi Police PCR van near the Sabji Mandi post office: 'Whoever has a bottle of the drink, please deposit it with us. These are not drink. These are poison.'

She met Habib photographer near the post office. He said, 'Please also get a report from the morgue in Baraf Khana.'

She was not in a condition to answer Habib. Holding her tummy with her hands, she started to retch again.

Habib said sympathetically, 'You don't look well. I have just heard that in Haiderpur, some people have been buried in secret. They may be poor, but they have their honour. That's why. What's why. Who knows perhaps they will dig up the buried bodies.'

Without waiting for Vimala's answer, the excited photographer ran towards Sabji Mandi on the right side of the post office.

Holding her tummy, Vimala coughed for a long time. Will she walk to the Baraf Khana morgue in Sabji Mandi or will she take a three-wheeler?

She started to walk. Meanwhile, the news had spread all through Delhi. Standing in groups under lampposts, shops and road crossings, people were discussing the same thing.

'*Garib ka hi maut hain* (only the poor suffer).'

'Even they are the same people who drink.'

'More people will die.'

'They are still being sold as local medicine.'

***

There was a rush at the Baraf Khana morgue in Sabji Mandi as well. It was filled with people from JJ Colony, Malka Ganj, Shravan Park and Anand Parvat. There were some unclaimed bodies in the morgue. Even six-seven people failed to pacify a howling old woman. Her son was the only earning member of the family with five daughters. Now, the government will give just Rs 10,000 as compensation. What will they do with just Rs 10,000? Working in a cycle factory, the dead man took care of six people in the household.

The old woman howled, 'Now, to save the household, I will have to start cleaning dishes of other people. Taking care of this family, I have aged in my youth.'

From the crowd, some stray statements hit Vimala's ears. Somebody screamed, 'To save our honour, we should have performed the last rites just there. Twelve hours have passed without any food. *Abhi bhi maloom nahin laash kab milega*… (we still do not know when we will get the dead body).'

…It was the same scenario here as well.

Vimala posed her question to a group of men, who sat on the verandah, 'Where are you from? Where?'

'Jehangir Puri.'

'How many died?'

'Our own man passed away, who cares about the others.' Shooing away the flies on their faces with a piece of cloth, they answered.

Vimala asked again, 'Didn't you inform the police about the shops selling poisonous liquor?'

For a while, they looked at Vimala with their unblinking eyes. Then one of them answered in despair, '*Police wale kha karenge* (the police will not do anything)? You are from newspaper. The police are your big brother. They just talk and do nothing.'

...Fishing out a handkerchief from her khadi bag, Vimala wiped the sweat from her face. She had heard the same thing when she was in Jehangir Puri after the riot.

'The police did not do anything?' She asked again.

This time, no one answered. The black van of the municipal corporation stood next to the morgue. There was a rotten stench. Everywhere, there was a rotten stench.

Pushing though the crowd, she left the place. The sun was a ball of fire above her head. Vimala thought of her old mother, worried that she was alone. However, whenever Himmat Singh was home during his leave, he would visit Vimala's mother every morning. Perhaps, he went to see her today as well. There was nothing to worry. Whenever Himmat Singh was home on his leave, she had nothing to worry. From making chapatis to taking her mother to her favourite doctor, Qutubuddin, on Singh Sabha Road, he would do everything. He would even play with her autistic brother...

She jotted down the scene at Sabji Mandi Baraf Khana. Now, only Nigambodh was left in her itinerary. How would she go there? Getting on a bus at this hour was not advisable. They carried people like gunnysacks of salt.

Vimala hailed a three-wheeler and started towards Nigambodh. The rotten stench of the cold storage was everywhere on the body of the three-wheeler. It had the same stench as rotten rice.

Will she throw up? Retch. It was as if someone was beating her insides with something, like a hammer beating on a piece of iron. It was as if the veins surrounding her heart hardened.

Khak, khak, khak... she continued to cough intermittently.

A gust of wind from outside chilled her bones. It was a wind coming from Jamuna River. Look, there lay the river, like a dry bone, with the colour of chicken feathers discarded by butchers.

***

Paying the three-wheeler, when Vimala stood outside the gate of Nigambodh, all she saw was the crowd of people and police. There were also gun-wielding soldiers. Perhaps some minister was visiting. Look, at the high platform, someone's last rites had already begun. Perhaps the minister was here for this person. God, God, on small platforms surrounding the big one, the bodies of the poor people, who died from the drinks, were ablaze.

Nigambodh was filled with young boys and girls, men and women. Vimala did not understand why an entire village, with women and children, would come to Nigambodh to witness these burning pyres.

From the high platform pyre, and from the rudimentary pyres, emanated the same smell. There was no difference in the stench of singed human flesh. She had felt the same stench near the kathi kebab shops in Majnu Ka Tila, Chandni Chowk or Katra Ghashiram. Vimala walked ahead.

There was a commotion to bring a dead body to under the *chhatri* to perform the last rites. Look, there was another dead body being washed in the water of the river. Behind it, there was a group of dazed children…

Vilama had never seen so many people in Nigambodh before. Even when she had visited Nigambodh earlier for the newspaper, she had never encountered such a rush.

Vimala heard someone say, '*Sale*, everyone will go scot-free. The factory owner from Ghaziabad said it was from a unit in UP. It is all the doing of the UP police. What will Delhi Police do? Now, it's hot news. There will be some noises in the newspapers. There would be some drama to catch the culprits. Then the government officials will take a bribe and everyone will go scot-free. And people will forget everything.'

Vimala decided now she would have to finish her job fast. Himmat Singh will take care of her mother. There was no doubt. But she did not feel well. The retching feeling now was more acute than ever. Vimala thought it would have been nice if Himmat Singh were with her right now.

Pulling the notebook from her bag, she jotted down a few things about Nigambodh. She sat on a wooden bench outside and wrote. Then she walked ahead and stood near the huge godown where firewood was stored. The door was open. The firewood, stored in stakes, was depleting fast. Today, there was a mob outside this shop as well. This she had heard at Hindu Rao Hospital.

She heard that there was a skirmish concerning the inflated price of firewood at the Azadpur Crematorium. Men had turned to beasts. How could they let go the chance to earn some profit?

Now, Vimala tried to enter the first room of the office. Today, there was a rush here as well. There was no way she could enter the room. She stood outside the door for a long time.

'FIR!'

'Death certificate!'

'Rs 380 for three quintals of firewood.'

'Pucca receipt, ration card? Permanent residence?'

'If the man did not have a job, keep the space under employment blank.'

'Signature of the informant? Deputy Registrar's signature?'

The sentences flew around. There was the rotten smell. Most of the people who lived in jhuggis (slum dwellings) came barefoot. Only a few wore rubber chappals, dirty pajama-kurtas. Some wore tehmat like lungis.

Even pushing and shoving, Vimala could not reach near the wooden desk. The crowd spilled over the old, discoloured desk. ...Look, from the very spot, Vimala noticed a dead body on a boat. She averted her gaze. She was exhausted. She has been fighting the entire day.

Faraway, she noticed another group making their way towards the crematorium. Her eyes darted away. Somebody had written on the wall: 'Do a good deed every day and you will receive a boon from God.'

Some people on the ground looked at the writing. Look, look, the mob was coming this way. Some had returned after the fire on the funeral pyre had exhausted. Though the tree stumps were still burning, there was a layer of white ash on them. She counted on her fingertips. There were 72 concrete platforms for funeral pyres. Today, all the dead were the victims of the poisonous hooch, the unfortunate men, who wanted to enjoy during Diwali. Tailors, sweepers, vegetable vendors, rickshawwallas, construction workers, labourers, cobblers, three-wheeler drivers... Only the man, who was placed on the high platform, was killed by the bullet of a terrorist. The minister had not left yet. The police and the civilians jostled together.

Look. Who was that coming towards her breathlessly? Arre, the man was coming towards her. Behind him were other people, as if they would just fall on her.

'Madam! Madam!'

Vimala was surprised. This, this was Ismail Sheikh. He was delirious.

'What happened? What happened?' Vimala screamed.

Ismail screeched, 'Madam, Himmat Singh mar gaya. Himmat Singh is dead. ...*Diwali ke din bohut piya, bohut piya* (on Diwali day, he drank a lot, a lot). Around 11, we brought him to Hindu Rao. He died on the way.'

Vimala started to shake all over. Look, there was his father. Daya Singh mochi, bereft of a part of his intestines. And, his hair? His hair? Vimala could not stand anymore. She sat down.

***

Life was like this. Those were the true scenes from Nigambodh in Delhi. Whimpering, Vimala said, 'Yes, yes, this is the truth. The truth.'

Next to her was Ismail Sheikh. What was he saying? What?

'What was he saying?'

'Himmat Singh's dead body has arrived.'

***

POSTSCRIPT

One week later, someone knocked on Vimala's door at night. Opening the door, she noticed Kashinath, hiding his face in the dark. He did not have the liquor bottle wrapped in a paper under his arm. But from the man emanated a rotten smell. Standing there, he said, 'His friends forced the drinks on him. He had a job in the *fauj* and they were jealous. Who is happy these days seeing someone having two meals with honest work...?'

Vimala said, 'Just say whatever you have come to say.'

'Listen, Vimala, after the shopkeeper gave my name to the police to malign my name, they locked me up for two days. I was shamed. I was shamed. As I was not guilty in any way, I got bail. If I cannot sell every piece of the dog's dishes, my name is not Kashinath. Listen, Vimala, listen, you stop worrying about these people in the slums. *Woh log naali ke kide hain, naali mein hi rahenge...* (they are the insects of the gutter, they will only live in the gutter) I had given away plots to the whole lot of them. DDA plots. They sold everything and returned to their jhuggis. Why do you suffer for those people? Why?'

Kashinath now approached the door. He said, 'You will regret it. God knows what kind of people you have to meet on behalf of your work. I care about your wellbeing. Leave all this work. I will make you an editor of a big newspaper. Vimala... You will get good salary.'

Vimala's patience had run out. Shutting the door on Kashinath's face, she went inside.

Then, what happened suddenly? Her head started to spin. The whole world started to swirl in front of her eyes. She screamed, 'Oi, Kashinath, you lusted after this body of flesh and bones, right? Come, come inside.'

Like a robot, he entered the house. ...But for a fraction... The closed door opened again and Kashinath fell outside the door.

***

First published in the collection of stories, *Abha Gardneror Abeli* (*Abha Gardner's Evening*), 2010.

Ishwari's Doubts and Desires

ONE

Ishwari Devi had heard that this time the members of Sri Dham's Ramayan Mandali were planning to travel to Janakpur. For this, she too had expected a letter from the member of the Mandali, Dharma Bahadur Rana. During the *Ramayan* Mela in Chitrakoot, she had met this young man. His wife had passed away in a terrible motor accident. Apparently, a lot of people died that day.

Dharma Bahadur's letter did not arrive.

Ishwari Devi was a widow. When she had met Dharma Bahadur for the first time in Chitrakoot, she had felt an inviolable attraction towards him. She had come to believe that one day she will be able to accept him as her husband. She was confident that one day she will be able to rebuild the life that had turned into a funeral pyre. This is why she was hoping that this time too she would receive an invitation to travel to Janakpur.

Dharma Bahadur was also from Uttar Pradesh.

The invitation arrived. She was touched to receive a letter from Sri Mahananda Shastri sir himself, who was like the guru to the Mandali. He did not just sign the letter written by a munshi. He had written the letter himself. Ah! Tears welled up around her eyes.

Shastri sir wrote with great familiarity:

This year, the Ramayan Sammelan has been organised in the birthplace of Janak-nandini Sita, Janakpur… You visit all our Ramayan meetings faithfully. I have read all the articles you have written. I was impressed with the depth of your understanding and your thought process. But as you have noticed, we have to give a chance to the speakers who travel from abroad and other states. Again, we also need to find a place for local scholars. You have observed how these scholars are so immersed in Ram-ras that once they get on stage, they don't want to get down. You must have noticed how we have to make time for these scholars immersed in the love of Sri Ram. This time, however, you bring with you a good article. In the birthplace of Devi Janaki, you will surely get a chance to read it.

We, all the Ramayan lovers, will gather at the New Delhi railway station on 28 November. Then we will travel to Patna on Magadh Express. Starting at 7.30 in the afternoon, we will reach Patna by 10.30 in the morning. There the Sri Ram Mandir and the Nagar Palika will organise a welcome meeting. The foreign scholars devoted to Sri Ram will be introduced at the meeting.

This time, you will also be there. From Patna we will travel to Raxaul. There, they will check the passports of the foreign scholars. After clearing immigration, we will reach Birganj. At Birganj, we will be welcomed by the workers from the other side. From there, Janakpur is just four hours away. ...It's winter now. You will get to see the snows of the Himalayas. Carry warm clothing and blankets with you. Let Sri Sri Ramchandra fulfil all your wishes! ...'

Regards
Your well-wisher, Shastri
Gurukul Dham, Dist...

Shastri Maharaj had never written such a long mail. In the last three years, for the *Ramayan* Melas in Chitrakoot, Ayodhya and Ujjain, she had only received printed invitations. Under the invitation, there was just his signature, and today, he had invited her with such a long letter?

She carefully folded the letter and kept it aside. Ishwari had no doubts that Sri Mahananda Shastri Maharaj had read her articles written in English, which she had sent to him three years ago, only recently. Now, he had understood her feelings. Perhaps he was also feeling guilty for not being able to give her a chance to read her articles in the previous conferences.

Issh... Issh... Guilt?

Do even wise men feel guilty?

Again, Ishwari's heart was filled with respect for Shastri Maharaj. To read the letter again later, she kept it inside her blouse.

...Like a lightning strike, Ishwari remembered Dharma Bahadur Rana, who had gone to Chitrakoot, Ayodhya and Ujjain with the Ramayan Mandali. Will he travel with the Mandali this time too? The way they give airfare to the *Ramayan* scholars from Russia, Thailand, Belgium, New York, London, Malaysia, Java, will they give him airfare too?

He was Shastri Maharaj's most favourite person. And why not? How important and impressive was the speech he gave on the development and growth of *Adi Ramayan*! She was impressed with the scholarship of the man who offered a comparative study of Indonesia's *Ramayan Kakawin*, and local *Ramayan* texts from Java, Malaysia, Burma. People say he had found the first translation of Goswami Tulsidas's *Ramayan*, which was in the custody of the Scottish Church College. He also discovered several rare manuscripts, which Growse Sahib had left in Mathura during his translation of the *Ramcharitmanas*.

Ishwari seriously considered whether Dharma Bahadur Rana was really a devotee of Ram. In the Ayodhya Mela, it seemed he said he will become a devotee of Ram the day he could prove that Ram was a historical figure. In *Taittiriya Aranyaka*, there is story of a devotee who did not eat meat for a whole year, did not sleep with women, did not drink water from an earthen pot to have Ram, meaning a son, yet in *Taittiriya Samhita*, the Ram turns into a prostitute called Rama. *Aitareya Brahmana*'s Brahmin Ram, *Rigveda*'s Emperor Ram, *Jaiminiya Upanishad*'s philosopher Ram… from among these thousand different Rams, would it be possible to find the skeleton of the historical Ram? Impossible! Impossible? Yet, Dharma Bahadur Rana continued to dig the mysterious tunnel among manuscripts and copper plates.

Ishwari was convinced that somewhere in a secret room within his heart, there was condensed devotion to Ram. Otherwise, where did he find the strength to work so hard?

Ishwari could not imagine Rana to be just a dry-witted scholar. From the moment she had laid her eyes on him, she had felt an inexplicable pull towards him. She was convinced that scholarship and the soul of a great man were mingled inside his heart. While travelling with the Ramayan Mandali in Chitrakoot, Ayodhya, Ujjain, she had met several dry-witted scholars who were climbing the tainted hills of pride. …Iss, iss, once trying to make a conversation with such a scholar in Ayodhya, she was embarrassed, even thinking about it made her say, 'Open up, Mother Earth, let me hide within you'.

Slowly, Ishwari had developed a kind of disgust for this kind of scholars. As if, there were no difference between these scholars atop the hill of pride, and a butcher. Scholars who had no love for humanity, there were just dead bodies inside their coffins. However, the comparison felt foolish to Ishwari. As if, someone whispered in Ishwari's ears, a person can be a big scholar, but it's not necessary that he will also be a good human being.

Impossible. Impossible.

This was the reality. Some scholars were like butchers. They wanted to cut up and examine the insides of the people who were less intelligent than them. Ishwari had met people like that in Chitrakoot, Ayodhya, Ujjain. …No, no, Dharma Bahadur Rana could not be like that.

The letter from Sri Sri Mahananda Shastri started to hurt the softness in her heart. Ishwari was excited beyond reason to be part of the Shashtri sir's Mandali. She longed to meet Dharma Bahadur Rana once again.

There were no hurdles. In this whole wide world, Ishwari was alone.

Ishwari's mother was from Ukiam, on the south side of the river Brahmaputra. Her father was a Jajmani Brahmin from Uttar Pradesh. While doing Jajmani, he had met Ishwari's mother in Ukiam. She was born in Munshiganj. After they fell into dire poverty, the family finally joined a carpet factory in Bhadohi. All her brothers and sisters worked in the carpet factory. As she was good in studies, her father had sent her to school. At home, all the children read *Ramcharitmanas*. She knew how to recite the dohas, chopais of the *Ramcharit*. After clearing all the Rashtrabhasa exams, she had joined as a teacher in a school run by a Dalit organisation in Delhi. Most of the salary she received, she sent to her father who lived in a barrack in the carpet factory in Bhadohi. The Dalit organisation had given her a barsati to stay. The barsati was so small that one could mistake it for a miyani.

She studied *Ramayan* with dedication. Wherever there was a *Ramayan* Pravachan, she would be there.

...One day, she got married to a teacher from the same organisation. During the Delhi riots in 1984, trying to save a Sikh child from a fire, her husband passed away. The Sikh child was studying Rasthrabhasa.

For this attraction she felt towards Dharma Bahadur, soon after her husband's death, she was filled with guilt and remorse.

TWO

Ishwari was at platform number six at New Delhi Railway Station, before it was seven in the evening, to catch the Magadh Express. She wore an overcoat. The coat was quite old. She did not have the money to buy a new one. She had a khadi bag on her shoulders. She had all her papers and pens and pencils neatly arranged in the bag. She had written a long article titled 'The First Raga of Janakpur's Sita' to read at this international seminar. She had referred to a lot of books to write the article. She was certain that since Shastri Maharaj himself wrote the letter and asked her to prepare an article, this time, she surely would get a chance to read her paper. To make sure that the article was not lost, she had made two copies of it. She had one of the copies in the khadi bag and the other in the canvas bag along with her clothes.

Pushing against the rush, she looked for the people from Shastriji's organisation. ...Meanwhile, the Magadh Express arrived on the platform. In the ensuing rush, it was almost impossible to take a step forward. Desperately, Ishwari went from one coach to another looking for the people from the organisation. She did not see anyone in the first class coaches. While looking around among the second class coaches, she suddenly saw a part of Swamiji's saffron attire.

...In the push and pull of the travellers, Ishwari was not sure how she managed to enter the coach. Clutching the khadi and canvas bags to her chest, as she squeezed herself among other travellers, her heart started to flutter like a bird in a cage. Her heart started to flutter thinking that perhaps Dharma Bahadur Rana could not come this time.

...No, no, perhaps, Dharma Bahadur Rana did not come. She looked around. Look, there was the Russian scholar Veskovich, there was the Belgian *Ramayan* scholar Herbert Hondinh sahib, look, that's Dilen Sahib from Guinea... Look, look, the *Ramayan* devotee from Bangkok, the beautiful Srisurang Pulthupia was also here. Ishwari was familiar with Herbert Hondihn sahib's blonde hair and enormously tall and straight Dilen Sahib's cheekbones and heavy-frame glasses... She was also familiar with Russian Veskovich's large body and child-like delicate face... Ah, who was that woman?

Ishwari peered through the crowd. She recognised her to be the British woman Elizabeth O'Hara, who stayed in Sanyasi Baba's ashram in Vrindavan. She had covered her head with the end of her saffron sari. Her long nose and bright blue eyes were clearly visible. ...Look, look at the sanyasi! With his one hand on the bunk and the other on a stick, he was trying his best not to fall in the rush of the crowd. He had an impressive figure. The other passengers around him shrunk into themselves to save themselves from the huge dreadlocks on the man's head. ...The discoloured blanket kept falling off from his shoulders. And look, that person was not a sanyasi perhaps, but a brahmachari. Even with the garland of rudraksh beads and saffron robes, his head was closely shaved.

Ah! Ah! Who pushed her, who did...? Ishwari barely stopped herself from falling on the passengers.

Finally, it was only after the train had reached Aligadh that the pilgrims from the Mandali settled down a bit. There was now a small gap in the aisles for people to move around.

With his munshi, Raj Tilak, pushing the crowd, Shastri Maharaj went up to each and every member of his Mandali to ask if they were comfortable. It was a difficult task to go to each person like that, but Shastri Maharaj was used to travelling rough. He has traversed many an uncharted road in the Himalayas, has lost his way many a times amidst the hot sands of the desert. ...After all that, wading though a crowd of people was not a big deal.

As Shastri Maharaj and the munshi approached her, Ishwari's heart started to flutter. She could not discern if she was feeling like this because she wanted to know whether Dharma Bahadur Rana was coming to the conference or not, or because Shastri Maharaj invited her to the international conference. By then, she had found a comfortable place near the window. Next to her was a family from East

Champaran district, with children and all. In front of her, there were several youngsters jostling for space. From their conversation, Ishwari had deduced that they were students from Patna University.

...Now, Shastri Maharaj noticed Ishwari Devi. With great concern, he walked towards her. The munshi pulled out a piece of paper and started to look for her name. Filled with respect, even amidst the crowed, she bent down and touched Shastri Maharaj's feet. In a gruff voice, laced with feeling, Maharaj said, 'Ishwari, from the very first day I knew you are a devotee of Lord Ram. May Ramchandra bless you.'

...Then the munshi whispered something in Maharaj's ears. He looked towards Ishwari and said, 'Ishwariji, the munshi is correct. There are three devotees from Belgium and France who have arrived in just one week's notice. They are our mehman (guests). If they need a place, please clear your seat. The munshi will find you another seat in the ladies' compartment.'

Ishwari nodded in agreement. Then she was afraid. Last time on the way to the mela in Ayodhya, she had to travel sitting on a tin box for 10 hours, without being even able to move her limbs. Even thinking about it made her sweat. Even then, she had to clear space for the foreign mehman. But, no, pushing away that fear, some other emotions started to create waves inside her heart. Almost shouting, she called out to Shastri Maharaj, 'Maharaj, Maharaj, has Dharma Bahadur Rana come? I did not see him?'

Maharaj stopped on his way. 'Yes. Dharma Bahadur and a party from south India have gone to Patna in the morning. We will all travel together from Patna to Raxaul.'

Lanky and little rough, the munshi almost dragged Shastri Maharaj away from the crowd and walked away. There was no time for chitchat. There were so many things to do, settle all the local and foreign guests, check their passports… There were too many things to do.

…Ah! As if a golden door just opened up in front of Ishwari Devi. Dharma Bahadur Rana has come. Dharma Bahadur Rama has come.

Then a sense of guilt overcame her… She has come to the holy birthplace of Laxmi Devi's avatar Sita and she was excited about something else… and what was it? Just the other day, she had jotted down the lines that a Persian poet had written in empathy for Sita's sorrows. At Chitrakoot Mela, she had met this student, Qutubuddin Mocha, who lived near Khuni Darwaza. … She started to hum the lines the Persian poet Ferdowsi wrote for Sita… True, yes, it's true. Only after her death, she was recognised to be a brave soldier:

Uske marne par hoth woh baat
Keh nahin sakte
Uski batana tab hota hai jab
Kehne ko stri hai, lehin bade
Bade bahaduron se badhkar hain.

(After her death, the lips cannot utter those words.

It is said that she was just a woman, but was braver than the bravest)

The woman next to Ishwari was feeding her baby in front of everyone, without shame and inhibition. She screamed, 'If you feel like singing something, sing it loud. We all want to hear it.'

Ishwari smiled sweetly. To whom would she narrate the excitement of her heart? ...Now, the train started to chug along faster. Amidst this crowd of water bottles, tiffin carriers, different bags of cloth and rexene, beddings, boxes, and old, young and children, this particular flow of feelings unlocked the doors of Ishwari's heart and came out.

...Like a reptile, the flow started to climb the fields faraway—the greenery and the mud huts. ...Look, there is a brightly lit field of yellow mustard, as if, from the sky, a golden yellow handkerchief has fallen on the earth. ...Those were the bajra (pearl millet) fields. Stacked after the harvest, the bajra straws looked like sheepskin, and those were the tilled fields. They looked like the skin of a deer. ...At some places, the straw was tied together in such a way that they looked like dead bodies covered with a mat, and those fires of straw were like the bursting fires of a funeral pyre. ... Perhaps they burned the straws to fertilise the field.

A mysterious feeling arose within Ishwari. She felt she had found a mysterious beauty in all these because of her unique state of mind. Dharma Bahadur Rana and the singular beauty of the field in Aghon, all these mixed together filled

Ishwari's mind like a psychotropic substance. As if, at this very moment, all these thoughts and feelings had turned into a jewelled necklace. Sri Ramchandra, Dharma Bahadur Rana and nature were the diamonds, rubies and the gold of this necklace, each one incomplete without the other.

Everything was preface! At this moment! In her heart, a thousand musical notes rose to a crescendo. …She started humming a song from Iqbal for the woman next to her.

Hain Ram ke wajood pe Hindustan ko naaz
Yahan ki shyam din ke ujala se adhik roshan hain

(Sri Ramchandra's existence makes Hindustan great.
Here, even the night's darkness is brighter than the day.)

…Today, seeing the fire on the field, she did not react. Yet until a few days ago, whenever she saw fire, she would start screaming. She would start pulling her hair. The doctor said this fear was because her husband was killed in a fire. Today, this fear was gone. Suddenly, her reverie was broken.

…She noticed how holding a bundle to his chest and putting his weight on a cane, unable to find a place to sit, the priest of Chaturbhuj Sri Ram Temple, Pandit Krishnapad Sewak, a man who was deep into Ram Shastra, was coming her way. Perhaps that no-good munshi was so busy taking care of the foreign mehmans that he did not have the time to look at the other people. Ishwari did not like this munshi person. She felt he gave importance to people depending on their influence or their money.

Seeing the old priest, Ishwari got up with a start. She snatched the bundle that the priest clutched to his chest and dragged him through the crowd to the spot where she was sitting. The priest sat down and started to huff.

'Why take such troubles at this age?' Ishwari wondered. At the very next moment, as if her ears were on the ground, she understood that it was the call of the soul. Anyone could respond to that call, boys, old men, youths. It was the call of Sri Ramchandra and Mother Janaki.

She then walked ahead and undecidedly stood in the middle of the aisle. She felt the crowd on the way to the lavatory could not pass by without brushing past her. The Bihari woman, with the baby on her lap, squeezed on her seat and made a place for Ishwari. With Krishnapad Sewak's bag, filled with a blanket and clothes, between her knees and her chest, she tried her best to get comfortable within the small space. Just then, she was surprised by another head with matted hair.

...Pushing the crowd, the *Ramayan* pundit Gajapati Mishra from Brahmakund in Vrindavan was coming this way. He was muttering something under this breath. He too was perhaps unhappy with the arrangements of the Mandali. He has been studying the *Ramayan* for the last 20 years. So, whenever he heard about a conference on *Ramayan*, he would eagerly join in, carrying with him his peculiar bag filled with old manuscripts.

Ishwari had noticed that in the crowd of all the scholars, at the conferences in Chitrakoot, Ayodhya, Ujjain, even he did not get the chance to read his own article. Perhaps he had not lost his hope as well.

At Chitrakoot, only a few stray beauties got the chance to read their papers. With bob-cut hair, high heels, lipstick on their lips, the women, who claimed to study the *Ramayan*, got a chance to sing a Tulsi doha on the same stage with the great white scholar from Belgium. Yet, the person who spent his whole life studying Dasharath Jatak and community *Ramayan* did not get a chance even after he spent the whole day, from dawn to dusk, next to the stage, waiting for an opportunity. ... She remembered. She remembered everything.

Ishwari got up again with a start and vacated the place for Gajapati Mishra. The smell of ancient palm leaf manuscripts and old blankets spread everywhere. The woman with the baby on her lap covered her nose and cursed under her breath. There was no place for Ishwari anymore. Pushing the crowd, she went a little further. A bunch of gun-carrying paltans was sitting near the door. They looked at her and returned to their private conversations. She returned to Gajapati Mishra and placed herself on the corner of his tin box.

***

She did not have any problem getting down at Patna station. She just had a khadi jhola and a canvas bag. It was, however, difficult for Gajapati Mishra, with his cane and the bundle of palm leaf manuscripts in his hands, the bedding covered with a blanket and the tin box. He found it difficult to carry all the stuff amidst the crowd. Ishwari went ahead and took the bundle of manuscripts from him. Only then could he alight from the train.

...Carrying garlands of marigold flowers, the members of Patna Ramayan Mandali and the station master were waiting for them at the platform. The members all looked well-fed. They wore spotless white khadi, with scarves on their shoulders and sandal paste on their foreheads. The station master was very thin. He wore loose trousers. As the scholars alighted from the train, along with Shastri Maharaj, the devotees from Patna Ramayan Mandali garlanded the visitors and sprinkled scent on them.

With the garland of marigold and with her flowing lock of hair, Ishwari too looked like a Sadhika. She was anyway tall and well-built.

There was a tent next to the station, where the meeting to welcome the guests was held. Meanwhile, Russian scholars Victor Sakharov and Pemila Lyudmila, who had travelled to Patna by air, had reached the spot. They too wore marigold garlands. Their bodies too were wet with incense water.

...Under the tent, Ishwari Devi noticed Dharma Bahadur Rana.

***

As the members of the Mandali got into the bus to Raxaul, Ishwari had hoped that Dharma Bahadur Rana would sit next to her. …But no, offering everyone the good seats, he, with the munshi, went to sit at the end of the bus. …It was a 13-hour journey from Patna to Raxaul. Would Dharma Bahadur Rana be able to travel like this?

Ishwari noticed that Dharma Bahadur had lost weight since she saw him in Ayodhya the last time. Now, he had a beard on his face. The beard actually heightened his masculine personality. Even the heavy-framed glasses on his sharp nose brightened his persona. Ishwari wished that she could sit next to him and somehow ask him how he coped with the grief of losing his wife.

Perhaps he adjusted himself to the situation as he was travelling with the Ramayan Mandali. She wanted to tell him so many different things.

Now, she no longer fell faint at the sight of fire. Doctors said, time did this, but in some way, Dharma Bahadur did this as well. Yes, yes, Dharma Bahadur did this as well.

***

…A woman called Christina, who lived at Barsana Baba's temple in Vrindavan, sat next to Ishwari. She had been in Vrindavan for almost eight years. Her hair was golden. Though she was tall and gangly, with her blue eyes, she looked attractive. She wore the sari covering her head, like the women of Braj. …She had already impressed everyone by singing the dohas from *Ramcharitmanas* and the chaopai verses. …Still Ishwari had doubts. Did devotion really bring her here? Did she leave everyone, her parents, and her loved ones, for Ram-bhakti?

…Then she heard the loud voice of Shastri Maharaj: 'Our foreign mehmans are requested to get their passports ready. We will have to go through immigration in Raxaul.'

Christina looked for her passport in her bag as she muttered, 'People are free since birth, why do you need a passport? Why, why do you need all these papers? Now, I want to become an Indian citizen, but…'

***

After lunch at Manihari, the travellers went back to their seats.

…The bus ambled along the beautiful landscape of the East Champaran district. …The mustard fields like a golden handkerchief from the sky… The empty bajra fields like the colour of a camel's skin… Even at Manihari, Ishwari could not talk to Dharma Bahadur properly. The women of the Mandali sat on one side. She too had to sit with them.

While taking her seat, Christina, covering her head with the end of her saffron sari, whispered to Ishwari, 'I don't want to sit near the men. You know why, don't you? Most of them crave for the warmth of flesh.'

***

It was already dark. The western sky was red. Then the sky turned into the colour of ancient ruins. Then the visible world disappeared into darkness.

***

Seven hours had passed. Suddenly as the bus reached Sitamari, everyone started a ruckus, 'Foreigners are not allowed from this check post! We missed the road! We missed the road!'

Then, Ishwari heard the gruff voice of Shastri Maharaj: 'What happened? Did we miss the road to Raxaul?'

The driver got defensive. He screamed and said that he had the permit and he could take all sorts of people through this road. ...The bus started again. The bright lights of the bus on the road immersed in darkness shone like the backs of buffalos coming out of water.

***

The bus stopped next to a wooden bridge near the border police chowki. A few gun-wielding soldiers surrounded the vehicle. Some of them peered at the Ramayan Mandali banner on the front of the bus.

...Shastri Maharaj, his munshi and a few other leader-like devotees ran towards the immigration office beyond the bridge. A part of the bridge was illuminated in the bright light of the bus. The huge wooden bridge stood like the carcass of an animal. This bridge was the border between the two countries.

Border? Border in the world of men? Ishwari felt that these borders in the human world were the symbol of human cruelty. Did the human race have the right to draw such borders?

Next to Ishwari, Christina, with her head covered with the end of her sari, was sleeping. Look, the garland of rudraksh beads on her neck was about to fall!

...Dharma Bahadur Rana was also among the people who had alighted from the bus. A little while later, huffing and puffing, they all returned. The munshi went to the driver and screamed, 'Not a single foreign devotee will be allowed through this road. Even with a passport, this is not the correct exit point for foreign visitors. We missed the road. We missed the road.'

There were noises and confusion everywhere. The travellers, all of whom were exhausted and sleepy, stirred.

The munshi screamed again, 'Let the Indians pass. But the foreigners? What to do with them?'

Then Shastri Maharaj's loud voice was heard. 'It would be better if we returned to Raxaul, even if we have to journey the whole night. We should not even think of taking the Indians to Janakpur, leaving our foreign guests here.'

Again, the travellers got into the bus.

***

Staying the night at a lodge in a place called Sitamari, witnessing the Gayatri tarpan that the sanyasis of the group performed at the break of dawn, and reaching Raxaul, filled with army troops at noon, all these passed before Ishwari's eyes like a dream.

***

The road to Raxaul was filled with cross-border trucks. They were lined up near the immigration office.

The foreign travellers were asked to disembark with their own passports. Shastri Maharaj reminded everyone that if they had something to declare, they should immediately do so at customs and immigration. The foreigners now collected their cameras and tape recorders. They decided that they should declare all the items.

...Ishwari and Christina went to have breakfast at a nearby dhaba. In front of the dhaba, there was a huge board. Ishwari said loudly so that Christina could hear, 'While entering India from Nepal everyone should read what is written on this notice board.'

They read what was written on the notice board: 'Carrying foreign goods from Nepal is prohibited. If someone carries Nepal-made steel utensils illegally across the border, they will be seized as per customs rules.'

...While she gave Christina company and loitered around the Raxaul immigration office, more often than not, Ishwari's mind was with Dharma Bahadur Rana. There were some problems with the passports of the Chinese and Belgian scholars. He was helping them. And, it was Christina who was sitting next to her? …Her sparkling blue eyes were running towards the foreigners' kafila…

***

The entry gate from Raxaul to Nepal was impressive. The doors of the ivory coloured entrance were beautified with brown flowers and vines. There were also pictures of elephants, lotuses and Goddess Laxmi. Sri Sri Shankaracharya had inaugurated this entrance.

Here, immigration was smooth. The munshi collected all the passports. The foreigners followed him. …When they returned, each one of them had marigold garlands on their necks.

The party reached Birganj at midnight. All the arrangements were made. They would stay at Rani Sati Temple. The Sewa Trust ran the accommodations in the temple.

This temple was built on the slaughter ground of a Sati!

Killing field! Siih. Siih. Why would she think like this?

This is the holy land of a pure woman. …In the temple, the marble statue of Rani Sati with her husband's head on her lap was bedecked with bel leaves and vermilion.

…As the other travellers ran towards the mattresses arranged on the floor of the guesthouse, Ishwari stood motionless outside the Rani Sati temple. There was a doubt in her heart. Was it a holy land or a killing field? She was fearful to look into the eyes of the marble statue of Rani Sati. She stood in the huge marble courtyard in front of the temple. ...Slowly the cacophony of the devotees subsided. Most of them had already taken over the guesthouse mattresses.

...Ishwari was not sure for how long she was standing in the corner of the huge marble courtyard. Suddenly, she came to her senses at the sound of a voice in her ears, 'Ishwari! Ishwari!! Why are you standing like this?'

Surprised, she looked back. Dharma Bahadur Rana was in front of her.

Ishwari could not give Dharma Bahadur an answer.

He did not wait...

Look, he was going towards the sadhak from the Dhanurdhari Ramchandra Temple. She had met this sadhak in Chitrakoot and in Ayodhya. In his wet clothes, from midnight, he will repeat Ram's mantras. There was the deerskin mat under his arm. He had dreadlocks. He had saffron robes. ...His body was all skin and bone. He removed the saffron robe and put it aside. And, even in the freezing cold, he sat down on the deerskin mat with his naked body and started to repeat his mantras.

THREE

Ishwari sat in a corner of the huge auditorium with other members of the Mandali. The meeting had already started. Shastri Maharaj had already introduced the members who were with him on the stage. First he introduced the foreign scholars with great pride. Then he introduced the members of the Mandali. In Ayodhya and Chitrakoot, she too was introduced by the Shastri Maharaj. This time, here in Janakpur, he forgot to introduce her.

Meanwhile, many scholars had arrived from Kathmandu. Now, she had doubts whether she would be able to read her paper on *Ramayan* influence on the first day. She even felt her own knowledge on the subject to be inferior compared to all those established scholars. ...She consoled herself with the fact she was already lucky enough to be able to hear the stories of these scholars' research. It was really a matter of luck.

***

On the second day too, the scholars embarked on their unique intellectual journey of the *Ramayan*. A group of aged scholars climbed the stage with a series of papers on the theme, influence of *Ramayan* in the building of a Hindu state. Among them were well-known names like Acharya Khemraj Keshav Sharma. There was a debate on the king as described in Rigveda....The caretaker of all men, this king stands still like the earth, sky and the mountain... The responsibilities of a king as described in Yajurveda... The picture of the subjects as described in Shatapad Brahman... The power of the people's organisation in Atharvaveda... The mantras from Aitareya Samhita reverberated through the hall...

Sitting in a corner of the auditorium, Ishwari listened to the speech Ramchandra gave in Chitrakoot. 'The king's path is the path to truth and righteousness. No religion is greater than truth. The king walks on the path of truth for his subjects.'

The question Ram asked Bharat at Chitrakoot: 'Have you been able to discard your 14 bad habits for the welfare of your state and your people? Fourteen bad habits?'

That famous speech from Sri Ramchandra: '...Janani Janmabhumishya Swargadapi Gariyashi...' Ram-bhakti from the Licchavi age... Ram-bhakti of Malla kings of the Sun dynasty... The story of the ancient Ram mandir on the banks of Bagmati... The role of the *Ramayan* in creating a Hindu state based on religion... She listened to Acharya Kshemraj Keshav Sharma's paper on the establishment of the Hindu state from the corner of the auditorium.

...Suddenly, Ishwari's head started to spin. She muttered to herself, Hindu state, Christian state, Musalman state, what is the meaning of all this? Are the countries, which are Muslim states, happy? Aren't fountains of blood flowing in the land of the deserts? The countries, which became Christian states, in Europe, aren't they fighting among themselves? What is the goal? Then she reprimanded herself for thinking such thoughts.

During the second half of the day, there was a discussion on *Ramayan* and the youth. Just then, Ishwari heard a youth from Trinidad scream out, 'These conferences are meaningless. These kinds of conferences have failed to show today's youth the right way.'

There were more words, which hit her like sharp arrows, 'Sri Ramchandra killed Bali by shooting an arrow on his back… We do not agree with whatever argument and logic the scholars are using to absolve Ram of his guilt.'

'…We cannot even accept the argument why Ramchandra killed Shambuk…'

'Shambuk was a shudra and Ramchandra killed him because he studied the Vedas. This is clearly written in the southern edition of Valmiki *Ramayan.* We need detailed study on this subject…'

…Now, three-four scholars got up and hollered together, 'The student hasn't read the commentaries on *Ramayan.* Valmiki never wrote things like Shambuk killing and Sita's entry into the ground…

Yes, yes, different communities have fought for Valmiki *Ramayan* like fighting for a dead deer in a forest.

Yes, yes, the Gaur edition and the North Western edition too do not mention the Shambuk killing incident.

'Oh, oh, read white man Butler Sahib… read white man Camille Bulcke sahib…'

Oh, oh, what were the students doing? …They will now break the mike…

'…A king like Ramchandra walked on this earth…'

'…Vishnu's avatar Ramchandra! Param Brahma's avatar Ramchandra…!'

Ah, ah, once they were on the stage, they did not want to get down… Did they have any sense of time? Ah, a bunch of scholars were still waiting in the wings to read their papers. Ah, ah, there will be a fisticuff now… On the issue of Shambuk's killing…

***

Despairing, Ishwari left the auditorium. …In her hand, the article, which she wrote spending so many hours, lay crumpled. …She tried to console herself with the fact that she felt a kind of peace in writing the article itself. It was enough. It was enough. It's okay that she couldn't read it to anyone. She got the opportunity to hear so many different things… It was enough. It was enough.

The headgear that Ram's mother wove for Ramchandra in the Malay edition of *Ramayan* is now the crown of Malaysia's Muslim King.

…She also heard about devotion of the Chakri royal family towards Sri Ramchandra.

She also heard different things about Sita's unique sacrifices. The picture of Ravan that Sita drew travelled to so many different countries… Kashmir, Simhala, Indonesia, Java… Ah, how many different shapes it took, the picture that Sita drew of Ravan? Did Sita really draw Ravan's picture?

…Outside, Ishwari looked for Dharma Bahadur Rana. The man had disappeared somewhere.

***

The sanyasis who had arrived with the Mandali had their own tent in front of the camp where they were busy with their activities. …While going to the auditorium, Ishwari had noticed one sadhu in a weird stance looking towards the sun. Now, she noticed, he was in the same position.

Hari, Hari, what was this terrible experiment on the body? Ishwari had noticed while travelling from Birganj, the Swamiji from Dhanurdhari Sri Ramchandra Temple had his hand in a bag tied to his waist and he was counting beads. He did not even touch a drop of water the entire way. Now, Ishwari noticed that next to the tents, which looked like camel skins, he was reading a bunch of papers, papers that looked like palm leaf manuscripts.

Perhaps, he too had spent a lot of time to write an article, but did not get a chance to climb on to the stage. He could not read aloud what he had written. …Ah, did he have any regrets? He had spread a few papers on the sun to dry. Did he spill water on those?

…Ishwari was not sad about not being able to read her paper, but she was heartbroken that Swamiji did not get a chance to read his.

***

As she reached the guesthouse, she noticed that many Mandali members had already returned. Ishwari was surprised. Look, that's Dharma Bahadur Rana! He was getting ready to go to Janaki Devi Mandir with a few women from the Mandali.

Seeing Ishwari with her papers, the two women from the Mandali, with their saffron saris, said to her, 'Perhaps you did not get a chance to read your paper. Do not despair. Even three women from our Mandali, who wrote an article after four years of study, did not get a chance to read as well.'

Ishwari could not say anything. They continued, 'Dharma Bahadur Rana will take us to Janaki Devi Mandir, Sri Ramchandra Mandir, the wedding pavilion, and other places. You should also come.'

...Seeing Dharma Bahadur Rana outside the auditorium, Ishwari was surprised. Why did he leave the conference? She was not certain. Why did the talented scholar of Sanskrit literature leave the auditorium?

***

There was a big rush of people from all over Nepal in front of the Janaki Devi temple. The wedding anniversary of Ram Chandra and Sita Devi was scheduled for this fortnight of the waxing moon. So, the temple was filled with devotees from places like Jajarghat, Chamghas, Bharatpur, Chautara, Gorkha, and Bidur, and even faraway Dhankuta.

...Standing in the immense courtyard of the majestic temple, with Dharma Bahadur Rana next to her, Ishwari felt a different kind of happiness. All her ill thoughts, the pain that constantly nibbled on her life, everything disappeared at this very moment. For this feeling that welled up inside her heart in the courtyard of the temple that the queen of Tikamgadh had built emptying her entire treasury, Ishwari again reprimanded herself.

...It was not so long ago that her own husband died and now she had feelings for another man! She was feeling this in the courtyard of the temple dedicated to Mahasati Sita. Was she an unholy woman? Were there other unholy women like her?

Dhang! Dhang! Dhang!

Dhang! Dhang! Dhang!

Carrying khanjuri and dhol, a group of devotees entered the immense courtyard of the temple built by the queen of Tikamgadh. Dharma Bahadur yelled, 'You go to the wedding pavilion from the back door. I will stand here. You can keep your footwear with me.'

...There was a rush near the wedding pavilion as well. The Ram-Sita wedding was just a few days away.

...A number of upstart teenage boys were sitting under the shamiyana (tent) next to the door. A group of youngsters were inside the ticket counter as well. ... Seeing Ishwari and the other women, they hollered, 'You have come from India? Today, if we had good relationship with India, this place would have been filled with Indian devotees.'

A woman from the Mandali asked, 'You youngsters have come to participate in the wedding ceremony at the Janaki temple, isn't it?'

All of them replied together, 'We are unemployed. We have paid the government Rs 35,000 to get the task of selling tickets to the wedding pavilion. If we cannot pay them the rest Rs 3,65,000 in 15 days, we will all have to go to jail. Our job is selling tickets and taking pictures.'

They continued, 'Among the 15 doors, the Indian government has opened just two. The rush of devotees have reduced to just 10%. ...Otherwise, do you know how much profit we could have made during the Sri Ram-Janaki wedding?

The woman called Bhaktimati asked again, 'Why are healthy youngsters like you unemployed?'

'We are the guys beaten by batons. We wanted freedom... We went to prison... Now, our blood is black like ink.'

...A rotten smell emanated from all the healthy-looking youths. One of them approached Ishwari and whispered to her, 'Do you want some help in carrying something across border. Don't worry. We have people in every police chowkie. Tell us! ...Even now, if you want something special, Rangabhumi, the playground of Devi Janaki, the place where the bow was broken, you understand right, the place where Shiva's bow was broken, our adda is next to it... Tell us. We don't care anyone. Our blood has turned black like ink.'

Dhang! Dhang! Dhang!

Dhang! Dhang! Dhang!

...More devotees poured in...

...More devotees poured in...

With the two women from the Mandali, Ishwari ran towards the wedding pavilion. Even during their sprints, the woman called Bhaktimati continued to narrate, 'Valmiki has described once this Janakpur was filled with flowers and fruits, this land, fertilised by the silt of 15 rivers. So many names this Mithila had, Vaidehi, Tairamukti, Jaynakheshtra, Krirapeeth, Vaijayanta and what else? With Sita's dowry, there were so many cows, rugs inlaid with golden flowers, kafilas of horses and elephants. There was also a paltan of soldiers wearing jewellery filled with multi-coloured gems.'

The other short woman from the Mandali added, 'Now, look at the people of Janakpur! ...They are wearing coats from China, caps from Russia... But their feet are bare, faces hungry...'

Another woman screamed, 'Yes, yes. They are hungry. There is no petrol, no kerosene, no business. Relations with India at its worst.'

'I heard that they had collected weapons from China...'

'You cannot survive on firearms, can you? Haven't you heard, the Chinese now can go up to Raxaul without any worries? Haven't you heard the other day a minister's brother say, if smuggling is stopped, the whole country will collapse like a house of cards?'

Ishwari had no interest in listening to these conversations. She wanted to return to the place where Dharma Bahadur was standing near their footwear. She had an absurd feeling inside her. ...As if, she had discovered a rare knowledge. That sense of guilt that was built up inside her like an impregnable wall was now on the wane. ...All the flow of her diverse thoughts had now reached a certain destination.

***

Even in the stone courtyards of Sri Ramchandra Mandir, Dharma Bahadur Rana stood next to her. There was a rush of devotees at this temple too, the devotees who had come to attend the Ram-Sita wedding to be held at the Janaki Devi temple on this month of Aghon, on the fifth day of the waxing moon. There was a huge crowd in front of the Ram Panchayatan, Laxmi Narayan, and Dasavatar statues. ...It was said that since the ancient times, the priests of this temple have been sanyasis.

As she walked towards the Sanyasi priest, along with Dharma Bahadur and the two women from the Mandali, Ishwari heard an ethereal tune being playing by a band party. It was the tune of the temple's band party. It was an ancient tune.

...Pushing the crowd, with Dharma Bahadur next to her, as Ishwari walked forward, she had the feeling that she was walking towards a wedding pavilion, that this Dharma Bahadur was her husband, and she his wife.

Dharma Bahadur her husband? Iss, iss, the widow was thinking such a thought next to the holy statue of Sri Ramchandra! ...It was an inexplicable feeling.

That ethereal tune of the band party, in her hand a garland of marigold, it was as if a wail burst forth, breaking her heart into two.

***

The two women from the Mandali prodded her, 'Move on, Ishwari. Move on.'

Even as she stood next to the Sanyasi, her mind was somewhere else, in a mysterious world. Next to the statue of Sri Ramchandra, there were small and big uncountable Shalagram stones. She could not concentrate on the scenes. Right now, her mind was a river, and touching Dharma Bahadur, it was flowing away towards some ocean.

She came to her senses in the sound of the tall saffron-clad woman. 'Maharaj Chandra Shamsher had built the ceiling of this temple with gold. Now, look at the condition of the ceiling! …Look, look, where they are throwing the garbage.'

The other woman from the Mandali asked the priest, 'I have heard that the temple is run by Guthi Samsthan. One can count the bones of your body, as if there were a famine…'

The priest, who was getting ready to perform the arti, said, 'The government gives us just four rupees.'

Another woman hollered, 'The boys at the wedding pavilion had screamed. Their blood has turned dark like ink. …A lot of priests from the temple have started stealing… Iss, iss...'

***

As they took a round of the temple, the band party continued to play the ethereal tune. Ishwari followed Dharma Bahadur like a shadow.

...The courtyard was filled with naked, half-naked sanyasis. Before everyone, there was a fire. Seeing this fire, Ishwari did not scream out, did not pull her hair. The bereavement of her husband's death during the Delhi riots lay asleep in some secret tunnel of her heart. Right now, this fire looked like the vermilion mark on Sita's forehead, not like the bloodied tongue of Chamunda Devi.

The Sanyasis were here for the Janaki wedding.

From Uttar Kashi.

From Tibet, from Vindhya.

From the caves in the Himalayas.

...The ethereal tune of the band party turned more mysterious. The smoke of the Sanyasis' incense had turned the pillars dark. The colour of their dreadlocks and the broken walls of the temple were the same.

The devotees lay scattered on the floor of the courtyard, wherever they found a place. ...Ah, those women, who were sleeping on the staircase, where were they from? Raj-Biraj, Birganj, Jaleshwari, Gaighat, Sirha, or from the faraway Virat Nagar? ...Look, some of them were cooking food in the courtyard itself. Some of them were packing their shops of glass bangles and vermilion, which had turned into the colour of the red earth. Look, those women were sleeping with their babies on their bosoms; their uncovered breasts hung like the nests of weaverbirds.

Ishwari had never felt the taste of this indescribable happiness before.

FOUR

On the fifth day of the waxing moon, instead of the conference hall, most of the Mandali members got ready to go to the banks of Dhanusha and Kamala rivers. Another party was going to take a dip at Laxmansar, following the path cleared by Mauni Baba. The brahmacharis, who had arrived from Chitrakoot and Ayodhya, had started their circumambulation before dawn. The length of the circumambulation was two-and-a-half krosh.

The brahmachari from Ayodhya was getting ready for a circumambulation covering entire Mithila. He also kept talking about a Labdhi Mahal circumambulation before the members of the Mandali.

Ishwari's mind was lost in treading the footsteps of Dharma Bahadur Rana. She did not feel like going to the auditorium either. Neither did she want to take another look at the article for which she had worked so hard.

***

As they found themselves under the giant banyan tree in Dhanusha, Dharma Bahadur Rana stood next to Ishwari. According to legends, parts of the bow that Ram broke still lay somewhere there. Ishwari studied the part of the bow, which was now a root of the tree, all the while remaining a shadow to Dharma Bahadur. At places, the part of the bow looked like two snakes mating; such was the wondrous colour of the divine weapon. Ants had covered some of the dry, broken twigs; they looked like rusted iron nails.

Ishwari bent down and touched the scattered pieces of the mysterious bow. It felt like touching rusted iron. People say there was copper in these ancient tree roots. Even while touching the pieces of the bow made up of the tree roots, Ishwari was thinking about something else. She had touched this holy bow of Sri Ramchandra, yet her mind....

All her thoughts were galloping towards a singular destination. Was Dharma Bahadur going through a similar experience?

Was he also in a same situation at this holy site?

...Look, Dharma Bahadur was also touching the pieces of Shiva's bow that Sri Ramchandra broke.

Ah, look, next to him was the tall, stiff brahmachari from the temple on the banks of Vetravati River. Touching the pieces of the bow, which at places looked like elephant trunks, he was muttering a mantra under his breath.

***

The Mandali's procession travelled to the bank of Kamala River as well. The devotees got down from the bus and set foot on the sands of the riverbank.

The brahmachari from the temple on the banks of the Vetravati River too limped along with the members of the Mandali. The brahmachari was short; his cheekbones protruding. He had dreadlocks and he was carrying a strange-looking canvas bag. The brahmachari was a talker. He said loudly for everyone to hear, 'According to legends, this Kamala River is the daughter of a Brahman, who lived in Mandarchal Hills. With tapasya, she had received a boon from Sri Sri Ganga. If you take a dip in this river during Makar Sankranti, all your wishes will come true.'

....No, no, Ishwari was in no condition to listen to the brahmachari's tales.

The river was shallow. The crevices under water were visible like body parts of a young woman.

A few travellers got into the river and started to play with the water. From the ghat, near the bridge, Ishwari too took a few steps towards the river.

...There was a ruin of a huge fire nearby. Somebody had lit a bonfire with huge tree trunks. The fire-eaten carcasses of the tree trunks lay there like body parts of a black bison. ...Like the body parts of a wild bison, some of the tree trunks were also in the water. The half-burnt pieces were turning under the shallow current of the flowing river.

...Ishwari entered the water and pushing the half-burnt pieces of wood started to play with the small fishes underneath. With her legs, she pushed the pieces away. But no, they would not budge. The weak current of the river could not carry them away.

Suddenly, she came to her senses at the sound of a brazen screech. The brahmachari screamed, 'Come out, come out.... These are the remains of a last rite.'

Last rite!

Last rite!!

Her legs were playing with the firewood that had gutted someone's skin and bones? She screamed and reached the bank as if she had stepped onto a poisonous snake.

Dharma Bahadur was standing undecidedly next to the brahmachari. He was soft-spoken. He was so soft-spoken that it made Ishwari uncomfortable. It made him cryptic.

FIVE

As the Ramayan Mandali returned to Raxaul, Dharma Bahadur sat on her right side. The brahmachari sat on her left.

To be able to sit next to Dharma Bahadur like this, Ishwari felt a kind of happiness she had never experienced.

The gods had afforded her the opportunity. The keys to happiness and peace were with her right now. Yes, it was in her hands. In excitement, her heart beat faster. This was the chance... This was the chance... Someone whispered into her ears, you would never get a chance like this again. At this age, you will never get a chance like this again.

...Another door to life will open again. There will no longer be the exhaustion of this brazen hellish suffering. She will now receive the proof of his acceptance.

...The golden sunshine of the evening filled the fields. The straws of the rice field turned into the colour of gold dust. There was a rush on both sides of the road. Some families were on tongas as well. With every family, there was a goat. Yes, with every family there was a goat. Some of the goats, marked for sacrifice, forced themselves into the laps of the women, the way children go to their mothers for comfort and shelter.

How could they sleep so peacefully on the laps of their killers?

What was that river? Feeding Janak-nandini with milk, made holy by the Kamdhenu cow, was it the Dugdhamati River? Or, was this the Goirika River, the holy site to perform the last rites of the ancestors?

...No, no, she did not remember anything anymore. Like the veins on the calf of a muscled man, the river flowed ahead.

...There were sand islets on the riverbed like pieces of meat on a butcher's shop. Ducks of different hues sat in circles on the riverbed like fishnets.

Hari, Hari, Dharma Bahadur's reverberated breath on her chest. ...From top to toes, she was drenched in an indescribable feeling, as if her body wanted to enter inside another body without leaving a trace. This exchange of bodies was painful, yet heavenly. Was this love then? But, love was beyond physical pain, love resided in the soul.

What was soul? What was soul? No, no, Ishwari had never found the answer to the question.

...Yet, at this very moment, all her thoughts, all her feelings were flowing towards the body, as if the body was falling in a river, like the eroding banks. Ah, body-like, what river was this? Each limb of her body started to speak and their voices mingled together. She felt a sharp pain in her bosom, as if the veins of her two breasts were alive and awake. The flesh of her bosom tightened.

The bus moved towards Birganj. ...The river showed its face again. Look, someone was butchering a goat near the river. The meat was on the bloodied skin of the dead animal.

Its own flesh on its own skin!

Ah! Was the same happening to her? Was her own butchered flesh gathering on top of her soul? ...Uh, Atma! Dharma!!

...Again, the muscles of her breasts hardened.

Suddenly, Ishwari noticed the brahmachari sanyasi from the Dhanurdhar Charturbhuj Ram Mandir who sat on her left. She was between them. ...This sanyasi, who said, who said, this sanyasi had performed tapasya in a dark cave in the Vindhya hills for 10 years. Did he achieve something, something great like the ability to conquer the body?

He sat with his body touching her's. All this time she had not noticed that her shoulder was touching the brahmachari...

Siih, siih, this brahmachari sanyasi now knew everything about her... Did he really know? People say these sanyasis can read minds. Did he find out about her feelings for Dharma Bahadur? ...Then he must consider her an immoral woman.

Immoral?

Immoral?

At the *Ramayan* Mela at Chitrakoot too, she had met a sanyasi from Giribraj. With a skin-and-bone body, the dreadlocks on his head looked like a fishnet hung out to dry. Everyone called him Hanuman sanyasi, for, wherever there was Ram Kirtan, he would be there. He lived on a machan in a tree.

That time, Ishwari was not in a right state of mind. It was not so long ago that she had become a widow. Climbing up the machan, she had sought the blessing of the mysterious sanyasi. Holding his hand up, he had blessed her. …What was surprising that a few days after receiving the blessing, she had regained the stability of her life…

Since that day on, she had a sense of respect and curiosity for sadhu-sanyasis. Since then she had received the blessings of numerous sanyasis at Uttar Kashi, Ratna Sagar, Ujjain, and now, now, rubbing shoulders with her was the dreadlocked sevak from Dhanurdhar Ramchandra Mandir…

He knew everything, everything—the storm that is stomping her body and soul. He had learnt everything. Whatever he must be thinking? That these sorts of people come to events like these as well?

What else could she do? Pushing away all other rational thoughts, a strong, meaningless feeling washed over her body and soul…

Her body was disappearing into the flesh of Dharma Bahadur Rana…

Look, look, one of his hands was resting on her thighs.

She could not dare to look at it. It was as if a scavenger bird was on an uncovered piece of flesh.

The body was now the language. Rana, who was speechless, quiet, now, now, with the language of his body said the words for which she had waited eagerly at Chitrakoot, Ujjain, Ayodhya—at each *Ramayan* mela.

Ah… The road to this journey in transforming from one body to another! What pain and beauty was this?

A ring on a finger rubbed her knees… What was this ring Dharma Bahadur Rana wearing? What ring? Climbing up towards her body, the hand would come down again… The ring would again hit her knee… like a mountain of sand on a river, a mountain slowly started to collapse. As if with great restrain, Dharma Bahadur did not want to cross the border of that mountain of sand. …That mysterious mound of flesh tightened again.

Issh, Issh, the Sanyasi was sitting so close to her! She could smell his dreadlocks, which smelt like dry figs…

Ah… The mound of flesh on her chest…

And this sanyasi?

As if on one side, there was a dry, barren desert and on the other, there was pleasure garden drenched in rain. On one side, there was an ancient ruin destroyed by war and on the other, there was a tavern filled with revellers.

Uh… He knew everything! The Sanyasi, who was sitting next to her, shoulder to shoulder, knew everything. After so much of hard tapasya, perhaps he had come to gain this knowledge.

Again, the ring hit her the knee.

What was this ring Dharma Bahadur wearing? What was this ring?

The ring that rubbed her knee!

It was dark now. It was dark everywhere!

A loud noise among the passengers jolted Ishwari out of her reverie. Everyone screamed at the same time, 'We lost the way, we lost the way. This is not the way to Birganj and Raxaul.'

This was not the way to Raxaul?...All the lights came to life all at once. The interiors of the bus lit up like a sunny day.

Slowly, the light revealed a hand and an iron ring in one of the fingers... The light... As if the light plunged a knife into her heart.

This ring, Dharma Bahadur was not wearing the ring... This ring, the Sanyasi was wearing the ring...

This ring did not belong to Dharma Bahadur... It belonged to the sanyasi with the dreadlocks.

The knife that the light brought forth went deep and deep into Ishwari's heart.

***

First published as '*Ishwari's Sanghshay Aru Prem*' in *Ishwari, Jakhmi Jatri Ityadi* (*Ishwari, The Wounded Traveller and Others*), 1991.

The Touchstone

ONE

In the beginning, everybody assumed that Dwarakanath was a simple man. People in the village gossiped about his taciturn demeanour… But when Gerryfield sahib gave him his old rifle, and also got a licence issued in his name, people started to notice a change in Dwarakanath. Often he would be seen in the nearby forest, with the gun in his hand… Gerryfield sahib was fond of hunting, and whenever he would go on a hunting expedition, he would take Dwarakanath with him. Those days, the sahib tried his best to make a hunter out of Dwarakanath as well.

Seeing how Dwarakanath reacted on these occasions, Gerryfield sahib would laugh heartily and tell his friends, 'One day, when I asked him to hunt down a hedgehog, how like a woman he pleaded before me. The fact is he will never be able to kill an animal. Even if he ends up killing something, it will be a human being, not an animal.' Saying this, old Gerryfield sahib had laughed again. He had no way of knowing that his words would come true one day.

...The elders said, with the gun always beside him, Dwarakanath lost his ways. They said his situation was like the honourable sage who lived in the Dandakaranya forest, as told in the scriptures....For those who did not know the story, it was narrated again, exactly the way it was written in the scriptures.

'While staying at the Dandakaranya forest, one day Sita told Ram: "You are a great soul. Yet, if one were to observe closely, you too have earned *adharma* (opposite of dharma, meaning immorality or disorder). You are free of this *adharma* only when you do not indulge in 'kamaj vyasan'. There are three types of *kamaj vyasan*—telling lies, adultery, and killing those who are not the enemy. The last two are more dangerous than the first. ...You have never told a lie and you never would. You do not carry the sin of adultery. You have never, for any reason whatsoever, lusted for someone who is not yours. But this third *vyasan* of killing animals without a fault of their own, now you have indulged in this *vyasan*. To save the sages of this forest, you have sworn an oath to vanquish the demons. Knowing this, I am fearful because I worry about your happiness in this life and in afterlife. When you would enter the forest carrying your bow and arrows, you would kill any demon you find before you. Because carrying a weapon makes a person proud—bloodthirsty... Listen, a long time ago, there lived a pure and honest sage in a holy ashram filled with birds and beasts. To break his long penance one day, Shashi's husband Indra left a scimitar next to the sage. The sage soon became so obsessed with the scimitar that he started carrying the weapon everywhere, even when he went to gather fruits. As he continued to carry his weapon, he forgot his penance and started to turn more and more warlike. Finally, he became so engaged in using the weapon that he turned into a warrior and indulging in *adharma*, he, along with his weapon, went to hell.'"

...Remembering the story, the elders in the village came to the conclusion that the gun led Dwarakanath astray. Since Gerryfield sahib gifted him the gun, Dwarakanath's behaviour had changed. Dwarakanath, who never showed any interest to any material thing, showed an almost indescribable lust for the gun. Seeing him pass by the road, the children started to snigger at him. Dwarakanath did not care.

...Finally, one day, Gerryfield sahib passed away.

On that day, from beginning to end, Dwarakanath was with the sahib.

The day was a series of tortures by the minor sahibs under Gerryfield sahib. Dwarakanath was uncomfortable throughout amidst the cacophony of noises. There was a time when this band of minor sahibs would stand before Gerryfield sahib like cats drenched in rain, alert in their military stances. They were all suspicious of Gerryfield sahib's volatile mood. Could Dwarakanath blame them? He himself had to face the wrath of sahib's violent temper. On occasions, Dwarakanath even had to bear the kicks of Gerryfield sahib's boots.

He happily accepted the violent temper, the kicks of the boots, because he was among the few who had also discovered a fountain of goodness inside the sahib…

That day, trying to remove the buffalo horn from the wall, standing on a stool, suddenly Dwarakanath had stopped. The group of the minor sahibs were laughing with such wild fervour that the entire two-storey wooden building shook like an earthquake. With his hands on the buffalo horn, Dwarakanath turned and looked at them for a long time.

***

Holding coffee cups in their hands, the two minor sahibs were again spinning juicy yarns about Gerryfield sahib. The energetic assistant engineer, called Mr Padmanabhan, taking a sip from his coffee, shouted in delight.

'Whatever others may say about Gerryfield, I can say one thing for certain,' saying this, he removed his spectacles with his right hand and added quite shamelessly, 'Once there was not a single beautiful prostitute around that Mr Gerryfield had not visited.'

After this, it was as if there was a fire on the crow's nest. Amidst fun and laughter, four coffee pots were soon empty.

The excitable engineer, Padmanabhan, started the whole thing. Following his lead, others joined in, and with juicy gossip, they turned the coffee conversation into a beer party.

It was the story of the women gang from Rajasthan.

There were other stories about the Oriya gang, the Dogri gang, all of whom were dragged into the conversation with all their delectable details. The shouting, the laughter, the mood of merriment threatened to cross the limit.

...Dwarakanath was sick of these goings-on. These people who, when the man was alive, would pussyfoot around, whose order they would obey without a word, before whose voice all other voices would die down; looking at their behaviour today, Dwarakanath was quite angry.

Yes, perhaps, all men came to this end.

Why Gerryfield sahib alone, so many great men were buried under criticism and hatred after they were dead, as if their deaths were more terrible than the common people, more cruel. Putting his head down and retiring from work for a while, Dwarakanath started to think about other things. Just then, on his glum, sweat-soaked face surfaced some clear intersecting lines.

...Meanwhile, few more sahibs from the company joined the party. The noises increased. Whether it was at the sound of their laughter or it was someone's leg, the coffee pot fell on the ground and broke into pieces. Now, Dwarakanath did something surprising. He got up. Running like a wild rhino, he came and stood amidst the revellers. With boiling anger, he pointed his finger towards a young engineer and shouted: 'Why are you making such a racket? You should be ashamed. Until recently, before the sahib, you were all like pussycats. You shivered like a diseased cat before the sahib.'

Saying this, he started to pick up the broken shards of the coffee pot.

From the party, someone got up and grabbed the collar of his shirt, but just that. What was expected to follow, punches and kicks on Dwarakanath's back, did not happen. Like some magic, the fire of the group, which was sitting in a circle with coffee cups in their hands, started to wane.

...A while later, they all went to their respective homes.

Dwarakanath gathered the cups and the saucers. Like the other days, the Nepali maidservant would come and wash them. This would perhaps be her last job in Gerryfield sahib's house. Coming out, Dwarakanath noticed that the Nepali maidservant was sitting near the tube well, with her head bowed, thinking about something.

...Slowly, dusk gathered. The mysterious darkness of the evening silently embraced the house. Until a few moments ago, the reality of Gerryfield sahib's parting had not entered anyone's mind with such intensity. Now, at this moment, huddling himself amidst the silence, Dwarakanath started to whimper in an unknown suffering.

Last evening, until this very moment, he was with Gerryfield sahib, like a shadow. Until this very moment, he stood next to him and offered him a drink. Working the whole day like a donkey, with an irritable mood, at this time, he would be like a baby. Like a best friend, he would ask Dwarakanath. 'Dwarakanath, you too have a sip.'

With his head held high, he answered, 'I do not have the habit, sahib.'

'Then sit there and smoke a bidi.'

'I do not have the habit of smoking.'

'Idiot.'

'Yes, sahib, I am an idiot.'

'Then you sit out there. The fact is you got to stay near me at this hour.'

...This was the first night of Gerryfield sahib. After that, he would sit there like the stump of a tree, dozing off until Gerryfield sahib's thirst was quenched, or sometimes, he would spend the time listening to Gerryfield sahib talking.

...Even for a single moment Dwarakanath did not leave the sight of the sahib, who would sit there drinking until midnight. At this hour, Dwarakanath had noticed a look of helplessness in the eyes of the lonely sahib. He had a feeling that this gruff, moody sahib was just a pilgrim sitting on the banks of a river with strong currents.

...It was the last phase of Gerryfield sahib's life. The flesh under his chin was protruding. His hands shook when he poured the drinks from the bottle to the glass, and he sat there alone and drank his liquor. Dwarakanath had a feeling the sahib was like a discarded old horse drinking water to quench its thirst for the first time.

...This way, sitting near Gerryfield sahib like a shadow during his favourite hour of the evening, Dwarakanath imagined various scenarios. In earnestness, Dwarakanath thought about another thing—if Gerryfield sahib had a wife now, he would not have looked like an old horse milling about on the road. Dwarakanath did not know anything about the sahib's past. But, now, after he had met the sahib, Dwarakanath thought it was not difficult for the sahib to find a suitable woman.

...Three years ago, the contractor who worked in Barsana had come to visit him. With him were his three beautiful sisters. They would sit outside and play cards. Sometimes they would go for a picnic, and during summer, during those sweltering days, they would visit the spot where the river took a turn towards south and bathe. Once when he had gone there to serve them tea, he had noticed that the women were not young, as he assumed they were. It was as if a woman's age revealed itself openly on such occasions. They had few articles of clothing on them. Their age made fun of those clothes.

A few foreign women had also come. They jumped around the pillars of the bridge in the making. From afar, Dwarakanath observed them and Gerryfield sahib.

...They were all lies. Those stories with which they made fun of Gerryfield sahib, they were all lies. Otherwise, Gerrfield sahib would not turn out to be a zero and one.

...That zero and one. Dwarakanath muttered the words inside his mouth for a while. Then leaving the dark rooms, he stepped out in the verandah. On the tall pama tree outside the house, an unknown bird was screeching intermittently. Beside this, the only other sound was the sound of the river, like the reverberating sound of a train in a distance. It was dark and the silence was unbearable.

Dwarakanath thought if the raucous party of the sahibs had lasted a bit longer, then perhaps it would have been better. If he had not changed the situation saying those things, perhaps, laughing and shouting, the party would have tarried here a bit longer. Compared to the clunky sound of the bird on the tall tree, the sound of the water like the sound of a faraway train, the fun and jokes, the shouting and joshing of the party was much better.

...It was the end of an era, Dwarakanath thought, sitting on the staircase leading to the verandah. After this, he would never be happy working in the company godown. ...True, the man departed just like that. Yesterday, Dwarakanath was sitting here, at this very place, like an animal mesmerised by Gerryfield's unfathomable familial look. True, yesterday, until this very moment. It was unbelievable.

The bird on the pama tree screeched again. Dwarakanath looked around. Then he started walking towards his own house. Though it was not winter yet, the cool wind that blew intermittently turned the drops of sweat on his forehead into tiny drops of ice water. Dwarakanath felt as if he was in some other place, as if he was walking through an unknown road.

TWO

After resigning from the company job, Dwarakanath stayed at home. Besides his brother, he had no one else. His brother's name was Kamal and he was a different sort of person. He would wake up early every morning, cook for himself and his brother and cycle for eight miles to the school where he taught. He was the sort of a person who would not sit idle even during his free time. In all, everyone who knew him had only good things to say about him. He was shy and he did not mingle with others often. Those who knew them both from childhood would compare them and praise Kamal while citicising Dwarakanath's irrational and inscrutable ways. Some even made fun of the way Dwarakanath looked.

While Dwarakanath too did not mingle with the others in the village, sometimes he would go and visit the old man Dewan, who once had property and power and who now lived in a dilapidated house near the three-forked road. Perhaps the old man's great-great uncle was the actual Dewan. Anyway, he did not care about the house, which was about to fall apart. Yet, he never ignored a chance to boast about his age. Whatever that may be, even the old man did not have many friends. So, he and Dwarakanath would now sit under the elephant apple tree on the road and talk for hours.

...Meanwhile, the villagers continued to snigger at Dwarakanath for being worthless and lazy and for living off his hard-working brother. Some of them could do it only once. After saying something to this effect to his face, they would look up and see his face, and they would swear not to utter such words against Dwarakanath again. Perhaps seeing the terrible reaction on Dwarakanath's face, at least for the moment, all of them were terrified. Later, those who noticed the terrible reaction on Dwarakanath's face would tell themselves, the man was a little different.

...Meanwhile, concerning his visit to Dewan's house, various juicy tales started to spread among the villagers. This was because the Dewan had a beautiful daughter. The girl had tied herself up within the house in such a way that people hardly even saw her shadow. Only when she went to fetch water, like a halo of light illuminating the way, she would walk towards the river.

In truth, people could not say anything per se against the girl, for they would always see Dwarakanath sit with the old man Dewan under the elephant apple tree. But everyone was convinced that Dwarakanath had started visiting the old man's house because he was attracted to the old man's daughter.

As he sat at home without a job, Dwarakanath was growing increasing irritable. On his visage were the constant signs of despair and regret. Looking at him, people thought he was capable of terrible cruelty.

***

...Then one day something happened. The old man Dewan arrived at Dwarakanath's house. Kamal offered him a chair. He did not take it and chose to stand outside the house instead. Dwarakanath came out of the house and they both walked to the clearing outside the boundary walls for a chat.

With great discomfort, the old man said, 'Something bad is happening in my house. Other than you, no one can help me in this case.'

Dwarakanath did not utter a word. He just stared at the old man and listened to him.

'You know that I have a daughter, right?'

This time too, there was no reaction on Dwarakanath's face; it was not his business to wonder whether the old man should have a daughter or not.

'You must have noticed her. I am very proud of her, you know why, not only in her beauty, now, even her thoughts are like a 60-year-old woman. Even at this age, her outlook to life is free of any emotion.'

As he spoke, an unnatural current of light passed though the old man's face. Something more powerful than the pride of fatherhood lit up those unfathomable lines of time on his face, at least for a moment. Dwarakanath observed the change on the old man's face with a cruel pleasure.

Then he said, 'Just tell me what you wanted to say. There is no need for such a long prelude. I know everything.'

'Yes, yes, you are right. Then the rumours about her, you have heard them?'

'No.'

'Of course not. You have no contact with the people outside. You are like a lone tree in the middle of a crematorium.'

'This means you are indeed very angry and like beating the mattress instead of bedbugs, you are…'

'No, no. It's not like that. I am angry with myself—I mean, there is nothing more foolish than trusting your children that you understand them. That's why I am angry with myself.'

'This means she has done something. There is no need for such drama. You tell me everything in brief.'

The old man wiped the sweat off his face. The lines on his nose displaying the signs of his age and the extra flesh under his chin trembled. Just at this moment, what this man was deciding was difficult to decipher for someone like Dwarakanath, who was imprisoned within himself.

'You can guess what I want. Finally, she is preparing to go and live with a sick man, and I want to teach her such a lesson, which…' As he spoke, there was a cold light on his face.

'I will show you the place where they meet. They have figured out such a place for their tryst if you see…'

After a short pause, he continued, 'In that place, filled with mosquitoes, age-old bamboos, thorny bushes, if I go and throttle him, no one will know.'

Now, there was a wicked laughter on the old man's face. For a while, on the weight of that laughter, the man's face bent down towards his belly.

Now impatient, Dwarakanath screamed. 'What can I do for you? …For some times now, I have this desire to see if I can kill someone with my bare hands.' Saying this, Dwarakanath started to wriggle his hands in front of the old man's face.

The old man gazed at Dwarakanath. At this moment, both looked like two childhood friends.

'I know, I would get this help from you. But, but, do you really feel like killing somebody? …Do you really mean what you just said? But listen, I am not thinking about killing him completely. Just teach him a lesson, of course, a lesson can be taught in different ways.'

Dwarakanath was known for not knowing how to smile. This time he smiled and as he did so, the old man's smile evaporated.

***

It was monsoon. As dusk fell, the sky started to gather clouds. A while later, drop after drop of rain started to fall. The atmosphere started to cool down. Wrapping himself with a shawl, and lighting the lamp, Dwarakanath sat on the bed. With his eyes half closed, he sat there comfortably. Slowly, the sound of the rain increased. The wind over the thatched roof made a jingling sound like birds entering their nests. For just a while, then there was the sound of the river eroding the banks. There was the forceful tandav dance of the rain and the wind and at this moment, Dwarakanath felt an indescribable happiness. Thinking how the change in weather could change the state of mind, Dwarakanath drifted into his reverie. ...He also remembered Gerryfield sahib. He loved such rains.

It was as if during weather like this, once could meet one's true self! Here, one could again find a way to review the most difficult decisions of life.

And, in this moment, one could find the deep satisfaction in crying, being close to one's self, for losing those precious moments of life.

...Again, from above the roof, there was the sound of the river digging up the banks. Now, there was no sound of the wind, just rain and rain! ...Just then, Dwarakanath heard someone press on the door. Yes, forcing the door with her entire body, like a storm, entered the old man Dewan's young daughter, Snehalata. Her clothes drenched in rain, turmoil was writ large on the small face plastered with rain-soaked hair.

It was as if Dwarakanath fell from the sky. She said, 'As my father is not at home, I had to come at his hour, under the cover of rain. I have heard everything... It would not do you any good if you try to conspire against me.' As she heaved slowly, her body moved like waves of water. Just for a moment. Then something profoundly sad filled her two eyes.

'You trust me... It's all true. All true... You have never experienced anything like this, right?'

She looked up and her eyes sparkled.

The gaze stirred something unexpected deep inside Dwarakanath. He stood up. ...Slowly, he walked towards the girl who stood with her back on the wall, like a guileless dove.

'Listen, Snehalata, I will do everything for you. Just one thing... you do for me too, just a little... not much... sure... meaning...'

'I don't understand what you are trying to say.'

Outside the rain poured hard and fast, as if it were the sound of some warrior's horse's hoof. Now, looking at her eyes, Dwarakanath tried to explain what he wanted. Trying to explain what he wanted, his limbs started to coil around him.

It was as if he was trying to release something painful from his heart. His contorted face looked frightening.

For a moment, Snehalata forgot her own state. She observed the changes in Dwarakanath's face. On her lips appeared a smile of hatred and ridicule. Just for a moment… The very next moment, she felt as if she were standing next to a snake. It was time for her to protect herself. Within the tandav dance of the rain and the wind, she left the house and started to run.

…The whole thing happened so fast and so unexpectedly that for Dwarakanath it felt like a beautiful dream. He walked towards the place where Snehalata was standing. He felt as if the natural fragrance of her body were still lingering at the place where she stood. The raindrops through the open door soaked the clothes he was wearing. Dwarakanath did not feel like closing the door anymore. Washed over by the wave of happiness he had never felt, Dwarakanath stood there at the very spot.

***

…The next morning, Dwarakanath went out. Leaving that precious feeling of happiness, when he stepped out of the house, the rain stopped. The dim light after the rain had spread a kind of murkiness everywhere. With the wind, raindrops fell intermittently on Dwarakanath. He enjoyed this despairing solitude around him… He had even decided to go and meet the old man. However, once he had reached the road, ennui and a fear of loss made him uncomfortable.

He did not want to go any further. For the first time, Dwarakanath realised that he was happy in his loneliness. He returned home. He spent the whole day alone in the house.

…Slowly, dusk began to gather. The light from the moonlit sky dispersed the darkness a bit. On the puddles on the road, light and darkness played their mysterious game… Even the gun slung on his back shone in the light. He walked towards the forest bordering the village. He noticed the two large eyes of a night bird burning like embers. Making a high-decibel screeching noise, the bird flew into a bush nearby. Dwarakanath wasn't prepared for the sound. If he wanted, he could have finished off the bird with a bullet. Gerryfield Sahib had killed several of those inauspicious birds. Later, however, the sahib had told him, 'It is not an intelligent thing to derive pleasure from killing these birds.'

…Yet today, Dwarakanath wanted to derive a moment's pleasure by killing the bird. Touching the gun, he stopped suddenly. Making the unholy sound again, the bird flew over Dwarakanath's head.

…He burst into laughter and fiddled with the gun.

***

Dwarakanath returned home a while later, had his dinner and went to bed. On his way to bed, Dwarakanath thought there would be another spell of rain. The rain did not come. …With the ominous screech, the night bird once again flew over the roof.

In the morning, like every day, after finishing his cooking, Kamal went to work. Dwarakanath got some oil and started to clean the gun. He started to clean the nozzle of the gun as if he were polishing a precious stone. Busy in his work, he suddenly remembered Snehalata's face. Then, as if he had found a renewed inspiration, he went on with his cleaning with more vigour.

...Was it even likely? Drenched in rain, a girl stood before him without any inhibition. Was it any way possible?

...He had seen a woman from this close for the first time. Twenty years ago, Dwarakanath would often dream about this blissful feeling of being with a woman. ...Thinking about this, he smiled. Twenty years were more than an eon. After those 20 years, women remained a mystery to him. Slowly, he lost the need for them. He got used to his lonely, flaky lifestyle.

...Twenty years was a long time. As he pushed away that unnecessary (later he had started to believe that it was all unnecessary) feeling from his heart, ultimately, it had all dried up and turned pugnacious...

This happened 20 years ago. He was then a 25-year-old man. Being 25 was no less wonderful. This was the age when one could not stand still under the weight of excitement and health, the age where no argument could convince the mind. At that age, Dwarakanath wanted everything to be unusual and exaggerated.

...Yet Snehalata's presence yesterday jolted him a bit. Whether it was some physical attraction or some filial feeling for that proud girl drenched in rain, Dwarakanath could not decipher. The girl was proud. This kind of pride hurt the feminine charm in a woman. If it were a physical attraction, it would be the supreme wonder of his 50-year-old life. It would be the wonder of coming face to face with his own self.

Dwarakanath got up. Carrying the gun, he walked towards the sal forest. The previous night's rain had made the place damp. The crumbling sound of the dry leaves in the forest could no longer be heard. Some part of the forest was pitch dark; in other parts, even where the setting sun was visible, it looked like they were covered in mist.

...This did not deter Dwarakanath. Mechanically, he walked towards the place the old man Dewan had mentioned and when he reached the place, like an animal waiting for its prey, he sat down behind a tree. ... Dwarakanath remembered what the old man had told him. This was the exact time. Sitting on one knee and placing his chin on the other, the way Gerryfield sahib would sit to hunt ducks, Dwarakanath waited.

The old man was right. Today, Snehalata wasn't there. The boy was. Braving the mud after the rain, the mosquitoes and the creepy-crawlies, he had reached his destination. For a fraction, a different kind of shame washed over Dwarakanath. The boy was young. The way Dwarakanath had a wonderful life 20 years ago, today, the boy was the owner of such a wonderful life.

...The gun felt heavy. He no longer had the same strength in his shoulders. The piece of meat dangling from his chin actually made him look old. This means, with the gun on his hand, he no longer looked handsome. Dwarakanath realised that this scene of him sitting on the shadow of the tree was really laughable.

He felt warm. Beads of sweat started to appear on his face. With great ridicule, Snehalata had looked at him and laughed.

Not exactly looking at him, but looking at his age. She had a killer smile of ridicule. When he wanted to make love to the woman drenched in rain, she had smiled that appalling smile.

The Dwarakanath of 20 years ago could smile like that.

This smile of ridicule from a woman was like a sharp knife, whatever it touched it left a deep cut.

...He removed the gun from his shoulders. He felt faint. ...All the blood from his body came to his head. The remains of the blood that would fire him up 20 years ago, it all came up to his face. Turning into a wounded tiger, Dwarakanath picked up the gun and aimed at very image of what he was like 20 years ago.

...What happened in a fraction!? There were noises everywhere, people shouting, and among them, Dwarakanath noticed the deathly visage of the old man Dewan.

...Though he did not remember what happened, he could precisely remember one particular detail. The fearsome bird with the ominous screech had flown past his head. Dwarakanath felt as if this ominous bird were following him for the past few days.

***

Time passed. The news that Dwarakanath killed a man was the topic of conversation among the villagers not for one or two days but for a long time, but over time even the memory of it started to grow dim.

...Dwarakanath had decided that he would spend the rest of his days in the jail. Inside the rough walls of the prison, one day without anyone noticing, he would have a normal death. This was what Dwarakanath wanted. ...For an old man, a prison was not really a bad place, if he could die there, he had reasoned.

...Meanwhile, Kamal got married. He had accompanied his wife Bakulmala to the prison to introduce her to his brother. It was the first time Kamal's wife met him. Dwarakanath observed the changing colours of the woman's face and her darting eyes, and enjoyed it immensely. She was not a beauty who could attract people at the first glance. But in her reactions, which revealed her state of mind, Dwarakanath noticed a great well of love.

....And then, this well of love immediately displaced that look like a dagger, those breasts like ripe fruits, those teeth like pomegranate seeds, and in the very first day, she appeared attractive before Dwarakanath.

Later, she got over her shyness. Carrying packets of laru and peetha she started going in and out of the prison. The woman came to Dwarakanath's life without any warning.

To him, who was looking for a natural death, the woman came unnaturally.

...Finally, even when he had decided not to count the days for her, he could not stop waiting for her arrival.

One day, he asked her, 'You will always take the trouble to come and see me?'

'Yes, at least as long as you are in this hellhole and as long as I can, I will come and see you on and off.'

Dwarakanath was terrified to carry on with the conversation.

While he had decided that the strapping youth from 30 years ago was already dead inside him, he was not convinced that in a dark room somewhere inside him, that dead man was still breathing. This was why he waited for the woman, who wanted to share his happiness and his sorrows. On those days when she would not come, even on those days, the very act of waiting was a pleasure.

...One day, the woman arrived to give Dwarakanath, the man who wanted to die inside the prison, the most surprising news. 'My husband has asked me to share a happy news with you. A number of prisoners will be released on the birth centenary of the Mahapurush. You do not have any bad report during your stay here. My husband said you too might be among the prisoners pardoned.'

With great expectation, she looked at Dwarakanath's face. She did not notice any change in his reaction.

'Listen, I don't want to try and leave this place, and no one else should try to do it as well.'

'You say it like you are upset with someone.'

Dwarakanath smiled and said, 'You will visit me sometimes and I will die here. As you can see, I am getting old. I would rather stay here than be someone else's burden.'

'I don't like that even at this age you are forced to dig soil with the other prisoners. You have your own land. You wouldn't be anyone's burden.'

There was such trust and love in her words that for some time Dwarakanath observed her reactions minutely. Yes, she was not acting. She did not have any ulterior motives to act like this. And, even if she was acting, Dwarakanath should consider himself lucky that he was given the opportunity to enjoy such acting.

***

Finally, her words came true. Dwarakanath was released on the centenary day of the Mahapurush. With anger and great despondency, he crossed the iron gate of the prison. It was already evening. The crowd of officers who milled around the gate was thinning. At the end, there were only a handful of them left.

On his way to dig soil, he had crossed this iron gate several times. But today, the feeling was different. Today, his very own flesh felt heavy. Yet, the playful young prisoner had told him, 'Uncle, the way you dig soil, it looks like you are digging it in anger and you get the strength because of your anger.'

Dwarakanath had smiled and replied, 'Anger is our enemy. Do you think this anger will give you strength?'

Overpowered by this very anger, this young, playful prisoner had done something for which he was now wasting his precious years in the prison.

Dwarakanath turned back. The young prisoner's face appeared before him. The face before his dimmed eyesight looked like the picture of a ghost. A sense of remorse and shame he had never felt shook the destructive foundation of his 60-year-old life.

It was the young boy who should have been released today. He is a strapping, green boy. He should have received the blessing of the Mahapurush. It was as if everybody was playing a very nasty game by setting the 60-year-old man free.

...On his way to dig soil, Dwarakanath had crossed this road many times. He had, however, not noticed the changes. He looked at the forest on the other side of the river. Those days, while accompanying Gerryfield sahib, the forest appeared mysterious to him. The forest now was sparse. Now, lights were visible in the forest. The light on the way, for Dwarakanath, the light looked like the white sheets over a dead body.

***

Bakulmala did not leave a stone unturned to make sure that Dwarakanath was comfortable and he did not fall back in remorse. She kept the household so clean and tidy that one could serve food in the courtyard itself. The house was so spick and span that Dwarakanath felt that unbearable and indescribable empty light among the household furniture as well. It would have been better if they were all covered with fungi.

There was another reason why Dwarakanath did not like this light. That young, playful prisoner liked this kind of light. He was always in awe of the prisoner, who was mad with lust for money and property.

As he was leaving the prison, Dwarakanath had seen the dark shadow of the prisoner lurking somewhere. That shadowy figure looked like a ghost. Now, this light, which appeared before Dwarakanath as white sheets over a dead body, for that young prisoner, it was the most desirous destination.

Finally, he had understood, there were other truths in life. There were other milestones.

***

Dwarakanath did not leave the house for the first two days. Putting his head between his two knees, he sat in one corner like an egret waiting for a fish. Only his two eyelids, which looked like broken nests of bumblebees, moved intermittently. As if someone had hurled a heavy object on a field covered with silt.

....The old man Dewan was dead, but not before making sure that Snehalata was married off to a respectable household. Sometimes Bakulmala mentioned Snehalata. She was happy. She had several babies.

Dwarakanath, crouched in the corner, perked up his ears. Even after Bakulmala had finished the conversation, he kept his ears open, maybe she would add something, maybe she would give him one more tidbit of news, news about the girl who had came to him drenched in rain.

But he could not reveal his wishes to her. It was impossible.

Bakulmala said, 'Sitting like this will do you no good. Why don't you take care of the vegetable patch outside?'

Now, he started to spend his days in the vegetable patch. He started to take care of the plants.

Bakulmala was satisfied with the new development. She said, 'I did not ask you to do so much work. You will fall ill, working like this. Now, come…'

Sweet were Bakulmala's words!

Dwarakanath started to enjoy it. He started to enjoy the morning sun in the vegetable patch. It was as if someone had filtered that sunshine with a smooth piece of cloth before sending it to him lovingly. This was how he felt.

***

Observing for a long time from the vegetable patch, and from his designated spot in the house, like an old sentinel, Dwarakanath was finally convinced that Bakulmala's attention towards him was not an act of fraud.

It was a surprising feeling for Dwarakanath to be able to think such a happy thought at this old age.

If the old man Dewan were alive, they could have sat together again under the elephant apple tree. The old man understood him. Unlike lot of other trees around, the elephant apple tree still stood at the very spot. Dwarakanath could have spent the rest of his days in peace and comfort. ...The way he used to feel when he had the gun with him, he felt the same kind of happiness. Yet, sadly, there was none with whom he could share this happiness.

***

... For some time now, Dwarakanath wanted to go and meet Snehalata. As the days went by, the desire started to grow.

...All of the old man Dewan's properties now belonged to her. People said she had a happy life.

For several days, he walked past Snehalata's house. Even earlier, she would rarely leave the house. Now, she was hardly seen outside. Like a young suitor hanging around his lover's house, for several days, Dwarakanath walked past the house. The more he went towards her house, the more he wanted to see her.

The man on the wrong side of 60 started to behave like a teenager.

After several days of fruitless waiting in front of the house, he was dejected. Just then, he noticed Snehalata.

She wore a small, tight blouse, the kind they wore in the town. In Dwarakanath's eyes, her small and rough hands looked ugly. If one cared to count, her age would be less than 30 years. Yet her hands were dry and rough like a 60-year-old. Dwarakanath remembered, the day she stood in front of him, rain-soaked, her hands were full to the brim, like leaves of sthalapadma flowers. Dwarakanath was convinced her hands did not look like this because she was drenched in rain; her hands were always smooth like this.

Now, he saw clearly that Snehalata had done nothing to hide this roughness of her hands. She had come outdoors for something. Once the task was done, she went indoors again, without looking at Dwarakanath.

Perhaps she did not recognise him. Yes, it was a long time ago; there was no question that she would recognise him. Even the idea that she would recognise him was laughable. …Despite this, he stood guard outside her house like a teenage lover. One day, she will recognise him. One day all misunderstandings will end.

In the beginning, he was doing it occasionally. Now, it became a regular affair.

Surprising! Utterly surprising!

Even when he was aware of the facts, the old man Dwarakanath could not suppress this hunger, his need to talk to her, at least once.

Finally, he started to behave like crazy. Ignoring everything else, food, sleep, he started to walk back and forth in front of her house.

Now, everybody started whispering, finally, at this old age, he has lost his marbles.

Then one day, all his turmoil ended.

It was raining that day as well. A storm was brewing, like the storm that had come on the day Snehalata had come to him. Dwarakanath was waiting for the storm to pass. After the sweltering heat of the month of Jeth, after the storm, the breeze was cool, as if it had had a bath in winter's snow. Though there were puddles of water on the roadside, the road itself wasn't muddy yet. Dwarakanath walked on. With wonderment, he noticed that a woman was standing in the courtyard of Dewan's house.

In the dim light of the afternoon, she looked like a shadow. Dwarakanath walked on.

In excitement, without any warming, his chest got heavy. At one point, he stopped.

She said, 'To be doing this back and forth walks for an old man is not only laughable, it is also dangerous for health.'

'Then you have recognised me?'

The shadowy figure, who looked like 60 in her 30s, started to laugh loudly.

'I knew who you were on the very first day.'

Dwarakanath felt encouraged. His rising heartbeats drowned everything else.

'Then you have forgiven me?'

She said, 'You did me a huge favour! You wanted to know just this much, right? …Listen, stop these walkabouts from today. You are an old man. You don't look very well too.'

'Don't worry. I wouldn't come again. Today, all my troubles are over. All these days, I was thinking, this weapon, meaning my gun, did not make me completely inhuman.'

Right then, Snehalata did something unexpected. She started to scream in a sudden burst of anger. 'Don't you have any shame to speak like this? You are a *lampat*! You are a *nara-pichash*!! I hoped that you'd die in the prison.' After the word die, the woman started to sob.

The evening light grew dimmer, as if someone had placed a lid on the face of a tunnel.

***

Returning home, Dwarakanath went to his designated spot and sat with his head between his knees. He did not feel like eating that night. Before going to bed, carrying a kerosene lamp, Bakulmala stood next to him. Looking at Dwarakanath's face, she could guess that something had happened, that the way she expected it to happened, it happened exactly the same way.

Bakulmala decided that this was her chance and she started to speak. 'So, you ended up meeting her. Wasn't I the inspiration because of which you could go to see her?'

Even in the darkness, Dwarakanath's eyes lit up.

'If I can tell you, I…'

Dwarakanath looked at her fearfully. It was as if he was a wounded soldier and he was hearing the gallop of the enemy horses behind him. The sound of the horses' hoofs on the gravel of the road caught him unawares. The simple woman before him looked like a terrible enemy for the remainder of his life. He closed his eyes.

Bakulmala started to speak.

***

First published as '*Parash Ratan*' in *Hridoy Ekhan Nodir Naam* (*The Heart is the Name of River*), 1990.

Glossary

Aai: Mother; also a term to denote respect

Aai chikau: Expression to denote disgust

Aapa: Boy

Aapi: Girl

Aera plant: Castor oil plant, *Ricinus communis*

Aeri threads: Aeri or eri silk is made by *Samia cynthia ricini*, which feed on leaves of the Castor oil plant. It is also known as Endi or Errandi silk. This silk is soft and warm and is popular for making shawls and quilts

Aghon: Eighth month of the Asomiya calendar; between 15 November and 15 December

Alta: Also known as Mahawar or Rose Bengal; a red dye women apply on the edges of their feet during marriages and religious festivals

Ambubashi: Yearly mela at the Kamakhya temple, celebrated during the monsoon. The occasion celebrates the yearly menstruation course of the Mother Goddess

Amlakhi: Indian gooseberry

Andha Mughal: Working class neighbourhood in Old Delhi, near Pratap Nagar Metro station

Atharvaveda: The 'knowledge storehouse of atharvanas', the procedures for everyday life, the text is the fourth Veda, but has been a late addition to the Vedic scriptures of Hinduism

Atlas tree: *Cedrus atlantica*, atlas cedar

Autistic brother: In the original, the word 'benga' is used to describe the brother. 'Benga' literally means speech-impaired. However, the description of the boy in the story (with saliva dripping from his mouth) reveals that he may be challenged in other ways

Ayodhya: Also known as Saket, the ancient city is believed to be the birthplace of Rama and setting of the epic, the *Ramayan*. It is adjacent to Faizabad at the south end of Uttar Pradesh. Ayodhya used to be the capital of the ancient Kosala Kingdom

Bakul: Evergreen tree with tiny fragrant flowers; *Mimusops elengi*

Bandar kekowa: *Mucuna pruriens*, also known as velvet bean or Bengal velvet bean. The touch of the plant, especially the young foliage and the seedpods causes extreme itchiness

Barabhateri: Derogatory word, meaning, woman with twelve husbands

Barafkhana: Literally, ice room; a mortuary in the Subzi Mandi area of Delhi

Barali fish: Freshwater shark; *Wallago attu*

Barpeera: Large-sized peera

Barsana: A town and nagar panchayat in Mathura district in Uttar Pradesh. According to legends, Radha spent her childhood here

Barsati: Small rooftop room or usually a one-room apartment on the terrace

Basanti Puja: Festival of Goddess Durga held during spring, basant; hence Basanti

Bat lamp: A lamp of either kerosene or mustard oil placed on the wall of a house

Bawna: Dwarf

Bel leaves: Leaves of the wood apple tree

Bengi: Idiot, also a term of endearment

Beta: Derogatory way of addressing a male perpetrator, to accuse him of something

Beti: Derogatory word to refer to a wayward woman; wench

Bhakat: One who follows the faith of Bhakti

Bhakheri: A dedicated room or place where rice grains are stored

Bhatara: A wild plant

Bhatkarela: Teasle gourd; *Momordica dioica*

Bhikhu Koomar: Refers to the job, not necessarily a family name. A koomar is a potter

Bhithi utha: Refers to someone whose ancestral house has been destroyed

Bhol: Sponge gourd or loofah; *Luffa aegyptiaca*

Bholuka bamboo: Species of bamboo that is larger in circumference and stronger than usual

Bhumichampa: Flower with medicinal properties; also known as Indian crocus, peacock ginger, round-rooted galangale

Bijuli bamboo: *Bambusa assamica*; a slender variety of bamboo used in making flutes

Boitorani: A tributary of the Brahmaputra

Bongora: Name of a place

Camille Bulcke: A Belgian Jesuit missionary in India (1909–1982), who came to be known as India's most famous Christian Hindi scholar

Chador: The upper garment worn by Asomiya women

Chandalini: Manifestation of the Mother Goddess, a form of Kali, in her most warlike form

Chando Sadagar: Rich merchant associated with the myth of Goddess Manasa, the Goddess of snakes. He was supposed to reside in Champak Nagar, Chaygaon in ancient Kamrup; the same locality where the current story is set

Chatiyan: *Alstonia scholaris*, an evergreen tree

Chaturbhuj Sri Ram Temple: The Ram Raja Temple is a temple in Orchha, Madhya Pradesh. This is the only temple where Lord Ram is worshiped as a king and that too in a palace, where a Guard of Honour is held every day

Chegun: Teak wood

Chhatri: Hindi, umbrella or a structure shaped like an umbrella to shelter a pyre at a burning ghat

Chitrakoot: A town associated with the *Ramayan*, Chitrakoot is a town and a nagar panchayat in Satna district of Madhya Pradesh

Dahi Mistiri: Refers to the job, not necessarily a family name. A mistiri is the one who builds either houses or wooden furniture

Dakhala: Name of a locality

Dandakaranya forest: Dandakaranya is a spiritually significant region in India, the place where Ram spent the years of his exile

Dasharath Jatak: The earliest version of the *Ramayan*, found in the Jatakas (No 461)

Dauk: White-breasted waterhen

DDA: Delhi Development Authority, a governmental organisation responsible for the development of the capital city

Deodha: Dedicated devotee of the Mother Goddess, who, on occasions, dances before the Goddess and goes in a trance-like state

Dewan: The originally Persian title of dewan (also known as Diwan) refers to designated government official or minister

Dhaba: Roadside eatery

Dhaleshwari: River in lower Assam

Dhekhal: Place, usually outside the house in a rural household, where the dheki (implement for threshing rice) is stored. This is where the rice grains are cleaned and rice is flattened and ground

Dhekia: Fiddlehead fern; *Diplazium esculentum*

Dhekuri: Female stray dog

Dimaru: Common fig

Doha: Lyrical verse format, extensively used by Indian poets and bards of North India. Dohas of Kabir, Tulsidas, Raskhan, Rahim and the dohas of Nanak, called Sakhis, are famous examples

Doloi: One who is in charge of a deul, a temple

Dom Para: Doms are the lower caste community, mostly involved in fishing, beside other trades; para is the locality; literally, the lane of the Doms

Duli: A large container made of bamboo used to collect rice grains

Durba grass: Dūrvā grass; *Cynodon dactylon*

Ferdowsi: Hakim Abu 'l-Qasim Ferdowsi Tusi (935–1025 CE), or Firdawsi, was a revered Persian poet and the author of the epic of *Shahnameh* (The Book of Kings)

Ganak: One who makes the astrology charts and predicts the future

Garo village: The Garo Hills, now a part of the Meghalaya state, was once a part of Assam. People from the Garo tribe would often visit the temple to collect the sacrificed buffalos, as caste Hindus did not eat buffalo meat

Garopahar: The Garo Hills; once a part of Assam before it became a part of the Meghalaya state

Gatala: Small length of cloth worn by rural women in Assam to cover their upper bodies. It is longer than a gamosa but shorter than a chador, usually worn by women, who, instead of wearing a blouse, wear the mekhela tied to their chest, covering their breasts. Until recently, it was the typical way of dressing among rural women in Assam

Gaurikanta Purohit: Brahmin priest who performs religious rites for his patrons

German grass: Also known as aleman, creeping river grass, *pasto alemain*

Ghantakarna: Bell flower; campanula

Goddess Laxmi: The Goddess of Wealth, consort of Lord Vishnu. Since Ram is considered to the avatar of Vishnu, Sita is considered to be the avatar of Laxmi

Godhuligopal flowers: *Mirabilis jalapa*, also called four o'clock flower or Marvel of Peru

Gohain Adhikari: Religious head of a Satra

Gohani: Wife of a Gohain; Gohains belong to the Vaishnavite sect, as opposed to the Sakti cult

Gomed: Hessonite, which is believed to ensure relief from the malefic effect of Rahu

Gutimali: A type of jasmine flower, *Jasminum taurifolium*

Hain Ram ke wajood pe Hindustan ko naaz: The actual couplet reads: '*hai raam ke vajūd pe hindostāñ ko naaz/ ahl-e-nazar samajhte haiñ us koimām-e-hind*'

Halfali: *Terminalia bellirica*, is a large deciduous tree common on plains and lower hills in Southeast Asia

Hanuman in Lanka: Refers to the incident when the Hindu monkey god Hanuman, with his tail on fire, gutted the entire city of Lanka in the epic the *Ramayan*

Hargila: Greater Adjutant, a scavenging bird species and member of the stork family

Hari, Hari: Lord Vishnu. Used here as an expression of exclamation

Hollong tree: *Dipterocarpus macrocarpus*; the state tree of Assam

Iqbal: Sir Muhammad Iqbal (1877–1938), also known as Allama Iqbal, was a poet, philosopher, and politician in British India, who is widely regarded as having inspired the Pakistan Movement

Jaimaniya Upanisad: A Vedic text associated with the Jaiminiya or the Talavakarashakha of the Samaveda. It is considered as an Aranyaka

Jajman: Comes from the Sanskrit *yagyaman*, the patron who hosts the *yagya*; here, householders who invite a priest to perform religious rites

Jalfai: Indian olive; *Olea europaea* subsp. cuspidate, also called African olive, wild olive, iron tree, and brown olive

Jalia: Small bamboo window covered with crisscrossing interwoven bamboo strips

Jamuki: Substance with which women's teeth were blackened. It is a glue-like smoke derived from the seed of a tree, which the recipient inhales through the hollow of a reed or a small bamboo stick. The smoke settles in the teeth, thus blackening it permanently. It was believed to be bad luck for the husband to see his wife's white teeth. The practice is now extinct in Assam

Janaki Devi temple: A temple in Janakpur in Nepal dedicated to Sita. In 1657, a golden statue of the Goddess Sita was found at the very spot, and Sita is said to have lived there.

Janak-nandini: The daughter of Janak, the king of Mithila in the *Ramayan*

Janakpur: Also known as Janakpurdham, it is the administrative and capital city of the Mithila region of Nepal and is one of the historical and religious cities of Nepal, being the birthplace of Sita.

Janani Janmabhumishya Swargadapi Gariyashi: In a traditional retelling of the *Ramayan*, Ram said these words after his defeat of Ravan. The literal translation would be, the mother and the motherland is greater than heaven

Japathowa parva: Ritual to celebrate the first menstruation. In Assam, the ritual is called 'a small wedding'. According to the customs followed in the Chaygaon region, after a girl starts menstruating, a japa, a round basket-like box made of either bamboo or cane, is filled with rice, banana, betel nuts and leaves and flowers, among other items, and is taken away from the girl's house to a neighbour's house, which becomes the groom's house during the ceremony. A girl who hasn't menstruated yet usually carries the japa. On the fourth or fifth day, when the 'bride' is given the ritual bath, the japa is brought back home

Jatadhari Vaishnabi: Literally, dreadlock-sporting Vaishnabi; female devotee of the Mother Goddess

Jatra party: Folk-theatre form of Bengal, which was very popular in rural Assam

Jeth: Second month of the Asomiya calendar, between 15 May and 15 June

Jetuli poka: A wild plant with bright red fruit

Kafila: Original Persian, meaning caravan of travellers

Kagazi lemon: Variety of lemon popular in Assam, longer, biggerand more pungent than the round lemon; key lime; *Citrus aurantiifolia*

Kakabori Satra: A Satra is a monastery of the followers of the teachings of Srimanta Sankardev (1449–1568), the Vaishnavite teacher, who is said to have established his first Satra at Bardowa, his birthplace, and then in different places of Assam. These Satras are usually run under the control of individual adhikaras (or satradhikars). In its basic structure, these Satras maintain a prayer house (*naamghar*), initiate the common people into the 'ekasarana' tradition and include them as disciples of the Satra from whom taxes and other religious duties are extracted. Today, there are around 898 Satras in Assam

Kakawin Ramayana: It is an Old Javanese rendering of the Sanskrit *Ramayan*a in kakawin metre. the Javanese form of kavya, a poem modelled on traditional Sanskrit metres

Kalapahar: Kalapahad or Kala Pahar (Black Mountain) was the title of a Muslim general of Mughal governor Sultan Sulaiman Karrani of Bengal. According to some historical documents, he was Rajiv Lochan Ray, an Oriya general of Gajapati Mukundadeva, the last emperor of the empire of Kalinga-Utkala. After he converted to Islam, he took a Muslim name, but is popularly known as Kalapahad. He was instrumental in conquering parts of Odisha for the Afghans of Bengal. He is also blamed for destroying a large number of temples, including the Kamakhya temple. Some scholars, however, believe that the figure of Kalapahar is largely fictional

Kalapani: Jail; refers to the infamous British prison in the Andaman islands

Kaldiya River: A tributary of the Brahmaputra

Kamakhya Temple: The temple of the Mother Goddess on the Nilachal Hill in Guwahati (also see Introduction, pp. 11–14)

Kamala River: The Kamala River flows through Nepal and the Indian state of Bihar

Kanduli: *Arius manillensis*, a species of marine catfish, also known as the Manila sea catfish

Keep her own japa: Denotes the coming of age of a girl, with the beginning of menstruation, which is marked with prescribed rituals; a *japa* is a round container made of bamboo or cane, used to store clothes and other items

Khabaddar: From the Hindi *khabardar*, meaning, a warning

Khalasi: Manual labourer; khalasis are traditionally employed at ports and dockyards, comes from the Arabic word, which means dockyard worker, sailor, lascar,etc

Khuni Darwaza: Laterally, the Gate of Massacre, it is located near Delhi Gate, on the Bahadur Shah Zafar Marg in Delhi.

Khutura: Edible plant that grows wild near roadsides; Spiny amaranth; *Amaranthus spinosus*

Kinaram Satriya: Satriya is not necessarily a family name. It may refer to the person's occupation, he works in a Satra, or his faith; he follows the rules of the Satra

Koch Behar: Also, Cooch Behar, the district headquarters of the

Cooch Behar District in West Bengal.

Kochu: Wild plant, some varieties of which are edible; elephant ear; *Colocasia affinis*

Kokila fish: Freshwater gar fish; *Xenentodon cancila*

Kunda flower: Star jasmine or downy jasmine; evergreen, branching vine, it isconsidered the epitome of beauty and purity

Kuri: Twenty

Lampat: Someone with loose moral character; mischievous

Laru and peetha: Assamese snacks made of rice power, sugar and coconut. The larus are round and peethas are flat

Lempur: Traditional silver anklet

Madan Chaturali: A ritual performed at the Kamakhya temple

Magadh Express: A superfast train between New Delhi and Islampur

Mahapurush: Literally, great man. The title is associated with the Vaishnavite sect initiated by Srimanta Sankardeva

Maharaj Chandra Shamsher: Field-Marshal Maharaja Sri Teen Chandra Shamsher Jung Bahadur Rana, (1863–1929), was the fifth Prime Minister of Nepal from the Rana dynasty.

Majnu Ka Tila: Tibetan colony in Delhi, established around 1960, part of North Delhi district between the Yamuna River and Delhi's Outer Ring Road

Manimuni saak: *Centella asiatica*; commonly known as centella and gotu kola

Manuh Pora Bakara: Literally, the field where human bodies are cremated

Markin cloth: Cheap variety of cloth. In Asomiya, markin also refers to America

Mati-kaduri: Edible plant that grows wild near roadside; *Alternanthera sessilis*

Mazar: Hindi, mausoleum

Mekhela: Ankle-length skirt-like garment worn by Asomiya women

Mekhela Ujowa Path: Long-winding staircase made of stones on the Nilachal Hill on the way to the Kamakhya temple. Mekhela Ujowa literally means lifting the mekhela. It is called so because the stairs are so steep that women have to lift the hem of their lower garment to climb up. Legend has it that the Danava king Narakasur built this staircase on one night in a bid to marry the Goddess

Methani: A covering for the breasts, in lieu of a blouse

Mora Pora Bakara: Literally, the field where dead are cremated

Muga mekhela: A variety of local silk, produced from the silkworm *Antheraea assamensis*, endemic to Assam. The larvae of these moths feed on *som* (*Machilus bombycina*) and *sualu* (*Litsaea polyantha*) leaves. The silk produced is known for its glossy fine texture and durability

Munshi: A word of Persian origin, meaning a secretary or a teacher

Munshiganj: Historically known as Bikrampur, it is a district in central Bangladesh

Murha: Stool made of bamboo or cane

Naamghar: Prayer hall, usually used by the Vaishavite community, who follow the teachings of SrimantaSankardev

Narahari Mandal: One who keeps the land records and collects land revenue; not necessarily a family name

Nara-pichash: A race of demons in the mythologies. Nara-pichash means pichash-like man

Open up, Mother Earth, let me hide within you: In traditional retelling of Sita's disappearance to the underground, this are supposed to be her last words

Ou: Elephant apple

Paat: The indigenous silk made of the silkworm larvae, designed and woven locally. During a traditional Assamese Hindu marriage, a bride must wear a dress made of this silk

Palengi: Net to catch fish in still water

Pargana: Administrative unit during the colonial period

Pathan suit: Baggy kurta-like garment worn mostly by Muslim men

Patta: Land document

Peera: A wooden plank with short legs, used for sitting on the ground

Pravachan: Holy sermons

Pui: Edible plant; Malabar Spinach; *Basella alba*

Purohitani: The priest's wife

Ram Shashtra: The *Ramayan* literature

Ramayan Sammelan: An annual conference on *Ramayan* literature

Ramcharitmanas: An epic poem in Awadhi dialect of Hindi, composed by the 16th century bhakti poet Goswami Tulsidas (1532–1623). Ramcharitmanas literally means Lake of the Deeds of Ram. Frederick Growse translated the *Ramcharitmanas* into English under the title *The Ramayana of Tulsidas* during the 19th century

Ram-ras: Literally, the juice of Ram, refers to the devotion to Ram and his story

Rani Baha: Name of a place

Rani Sati: Also identified as Narayani Devi and referred to as Dadiji (grandmother), is said to be a Rajasthani woman who lived sometime between the 13th and 17th centuries and committed sati (self-immolation) on her husband's death. Various temples in Rajasthan and elsewhere are devoted to her worship and commemorate her act

Rashtrabhasa: The national language, Hindi

Rauta: Name of a place in Barpeta district in Assam

Riha-mekhela: Riha is an extraneous garment worn with a mekhela. It is longer than a gamosa but shorter than a chador. It is used when the mekhela is tied to the waist instead of above the breast. In such cases, the woman would wear a blouse, and will also cover her upper body with a chador, not a gatala

Robab tenga: A large citrus fruit, similar to a pomelo and grapefruit

Sadhika: The female sadhak, someone who follows a particular sadhana, a way of life designed to attain spiritual enlightenment

Sara: Evergreen tree with medicinal properties

Seelampur: Neighbourhood in East Delhi

Shalagram: Also, Shaligram, refers to a fossilised shells of the marine creature Nautilus, found in riverbeds or riverbanks in the Himalayan region. They are used as an aniconic symbol and reminder of god Vishnu as the Universal Principle.

Shambuk: Also, Shambuka, a character in some versions of the *Ramayana*, where, he, a shudra ascetic, was slain by Ram for attempting to perform penance in violation of dharma

Shatha Barat: A ritual performed at the Kamakhya temple

Shingari fruit: Also known as water chestnut and singhara

Suwari festival: Also known as bhatheli, sori, parwa in different regions of lower Assam; a tribal fertility rite in its origin, the festival, among other things, is marked by the erection of bamboo totem poles

Taittiriya Aranyaka: The Aranyakas are the ritual sacrifice part of the ancient Indian texts, the Vedas. Taittiriya Aranyaka has ten chapters, of which, one to six form the Aranyaka proper

Tandav dance: The dance of destruction, associated with Shiva

Tehmat: Also called tamba, Punjabi version of the lungi

The picture of Ravan that Sita drew: In some non-canonical version of the *Ramayan*, upon her return to Ayodhya, it is said that Sita drew a picture of Ravan on the floor of her palace to show her friends how fearsome he looked. Ram mistook it as Sita's affection for the demon and this is said to be the reason why Sita was banished

Three-Chowk Mirja: Also called Mirza, a town in rural Kamrup district

Titachapa: Magnolia, *Michelia baillonii*

Ugha-chereki: Bamboo instruments used to arrange the threads before they are placed in a loom

Ukiam: A village in lower Assam, on the south bank of Brahmaputra

Uriam wood: *Bischofia javanica*; Bishop wood

Vrindavan: A town in the Mathura district of Uttar Pradesh, it is the site where according to Hinduism, Lord Krishna spent his childhood days.

Wooden pera: Large wooden box, used to store valuables

Xhiki, adheli: Literally loose change; xhiki is a 25 paise coin and adheli is a 50 paise coin

Xilikha: *Terminalia chebula*, commonly known as black- or chebulic myrobalan, is a species of Terminalia, native to South Asia. It is the main ingredient in the Ayurvedic formulation Triphala which is used for kidney and liver dysfunctions

Yajurveda: The Veda of prose mantras, it is a compilation of ritual offering formulas that were said by a priest while an individual performed ritual actions such as those before the yajna fire. It is one of the four Vedas, and one of the scriptures of Hinduism

Chronology of Events

1942: Indira Goswami is born on 14 November, in Guwahati, to Umakanta Goswami and Ambika Devi

1954: Joins Tarini Charan Girls High School, Guwahati after early education in Latashil Primary School, Guwahati and Pine Mount School in Shillong

1957: Completes school education from Tarini Charan Girls High School, Guwahati

1960: Graduates from Cotton College, Guwahati

1962: Publishes first short story collection, *Chinaki Morom* (*Known Love*)

1963: Completes Master's degree in Assamese literature from Gauhati University, Guwahati

1965: Marries Madhaven Raisom Iyengar, a civil engineer from Karnataka

1967: Madhaven Raisom Iyengar dies in a road accident in Jammu & Kashmir

1968: Joins the Sainik School, Goalpara, Assam as a teacher

1969: Joins the Institute of Oriental Philosophy, Vrindavan to research on *Ramayan* under the supervision of Upendra Chandra Lekharu

1971: Joins the Modern Indian Languages and Literary Studies (MIL) Department at the University of Delhi

1972: Publishes first novel, *Chenabor Shrot* (*The Currents of Chenab*)

1973: Receives Ph.D. from Gauhati University for her thesis 'Comparative Study of Goswami Tulsi Das' *Ramcharitmanas* and Madhab Kandali's Assamese *Ramayana*'

1976: Travels to Japan and South East Asia

1983: Receives the Sahitya Akademi Award for Assamese for *Mamore Dhora Tarowal Aru Dukhan Upanyas* (*The Rusted Sword and Two Other Novellas*)

1988: Receives Asam Sahitya Sabha Award for *Datal Hatir Une Khowa Howdah* (*The Moth Eaten Howdah of a Tusker*); publishes the autobiography *Adha Likha Dastabej* (*An Unfinished Autobiography*)

1989: Receives Bharat Nirman Award for *Sanskar, Udaybhabur Charitra Ityadi (Sanskar, Udaybhanu's Character and Others*)

1990: Publishes the English version of her autobiography *An Unfinished Autobiography*

1992: Participates in an international *Ramayan* meet held in Indonesia

1996: Receives Kamal Kumari Award from the Kamal Kumari Foundation for lifelong dedication to literature

1998: Travels to Spain to participate in a conference on *Ramayan* as chief guest

1999: Receives Tulsi Award during a conference on 'Tulsidas and His Works' organised by the University of Florida in the US; publishes an omnibus of 12 novels in Assamese

2001: Receives the Jnanpith Award

2002: Rejects Padma Shri Award; receives D.Lit. from Rabindra Bharati University in West Bengal

2005: Appointed the chief interlocutor between ULFA and the government through the People's Consultative Group (PCG), a citizen's group in Assam, comprising 11 members and established by the United Liberation Front of Assam (ULFA). Retires from Delhi University and relocates to Guwahati

2011: Dies of multiple organ failure after prolonged illness at the Gauhati Medical College Hospital

Bibliography

Short story collections: *Chinaki Morom* (*Known Love*), 1962; *Koina* (*The Bride*), 1966; *Hridoy Ekhan Nodir Naam* (*The Heart is the Name of River*), 1990; *Mamoni Raisomar Swanirbasito Galpa* (*Selected Short Stories of Mamoni Raisom*), 1998; *Mamoni Raisom Goswamir Priyo Galpa* (*Favourite Short Stories of Mamoni Raisam Goswami*), 1998; *Abha Gardneror Abeli* (*Abha Gardner's Evening*), 2010

Novels: *Chenabor Shrot* (*The Currents of Chenab*), 1972; *Nilakanthi Braja* (*Blue-Necked Braja*), 1976; *Ahiran*, 1980; *Mamore Dhora Tarowal Aru Dukhan Upanyas* (*The Rusted Sword and Two Other Novellas*), 1980; *Datal Hatir Une Khowa Howdah* (*The Moth-Eaten Howdah of a Tusker*), 1988; *Sanskar, Udaybhanur Charitra Ityadi* (*Sanskar, Udaybhanu's Character and Others*), 1989; *Ishwari, Jakhmi Jatri Ityadi* (*Ishwari, The Wounded Traveller and Others*), 1991; *Tej Aru Dhulire Dhusarito Pristha* (*Pages Stained with Blood and Dust*), 1994; *Mamoni Raisom Goswamir Upanyah Samagra* (*The Complete Novels of Mamoni Raisom Goswami*), 1998; *Dasharathir Khoj* (*Dashrathi's Footsteps*), 1999; *Chinnamastar Manuhto* (*The Man from Chinnamasta*), 2001; *Tengphakhri Tehsildaror Tamor Tarowal* (*The Bronze Sword of Tengphakhri Tehsildar*), 2009

Autobiography: *Adha Likha Dastabej* (*An Unfinished Autobiography*), 1988

Poetry: *Pain and Flesh*, 2008

Biography: *Mohiyoshi Kamala* (*The Great Kamala*), 1995

Translation: *The Short Stories of Premchand*, 1975, *Jatak Katha*, 1996 (Goswami translated extensively from Hindi, much of which remains uncollected)

In English (translated by the author herself): *The Shadow of the Dark God and the Sin*, 1986; An Unfinished Autobiography, 1990; *Saga of South Kamrup*, 1993; *Ramayana from Ganga to Brahmaputra*, 1996; *Shadow of Kamakhya: Stories*, 2005

English Translation (by other translators): *An Unfinished Autobiography*, trans P. Kotoky, 2002; *Pages Stained with Blood*, trans Pradeep Acharya, 2002; *The Blue-necked God*, trans Gayatri Bhattacharya, 2013; *The Bronze Sword of Tengphakhri Tehsildar*, trans Aruni Kashyap, 2013; *The Man from Chinnamasta*, trans Prashant Goswami, 2015

Edited works: *Eri Oha Dinbor* (*Days that we Left Behind*, with Dr Malaya Khaund), 1993; *Indian Folklore*, 2003; *Ravana: Myths, Legends and Lore* (with Manjeet Baruah), 2009

Acknowledgements

The translator would like to thank Sabita Sarma for her generosity in allowing the translation rights to the stories and her goodwill for the project. Acknowledgements are also due to my friend J. Shashikumar who commissioned the first story for another publication house, to Sukrita Paul Kumar for her unfailing trust, and to Arpita Kuila and Madhu Raghavendra for their friendship and love. To Priyanka Sarkar, my guiding light, for being the kind of crazy I didn't need in life. Finally, thank you Nirmal Kanti Bhattacherjee sir for replying to my email and agreeing to go ahead with the project, and K.E. Priyamvada for the fine editing and the entire Niyogi Books team for their support in making the book. And to you, dear readers, thank you for giving this book a chance.

About the Translator

Dibyajyoti Sarma

Writer and editor Dibyajyoti Sarma has published three volumes of poetry (the last being *Book of Prayers for the Nonbeliever*), two books of translations of Assamese poets—Sananta Tanty and Kamal Kumar Tanti—and an academic book, besides numerous writing credits in edited volumes, journals and websites. He was born in Assam and now lives in Delhi, where he works as a journalist and runs the independent publishing outfit Red River.